Confessions of a Bookaholic

JOSLYN WESTBROOK

Joslyn Westbrook ♡

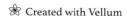

BOOK PLAYLIST

Everything I Wanted - Billie Eilish
Loyal - Drake
Shameless - Camila Cabello
Could've Been - H.E.R. (feat. Bryson Tiller)
In Between - dvsn
Should've Said So - Camila Cabello
Wrong Places - H.E.R.
Drown in it - Syd
Comfortable - H.E.R.
Anywhere - 112
Sexbeat - Usher, Lil John, Ludacris
Feels - Kehlani
Speechless - Dan + Shay (feat. Tori Kelly)
Braggadocious - DownNout
Final Fantasy - Drake
Bad Guy - Billie Eilish
Rock Star - Post Malone
Bitches Broken Hearts - Billie Eilish
Wasted Love - Jhené Aiko
End Up With You - Carrie Underwood

You can find the **Confessions of a Bookaholic Playlist** on Spotify

ALSO BY JOSLYN WESTBROOK

Razzle My Dazzle Series
Cinderella-ish (Book 1)
Haute Couture (Book 2)
Princessa (Book 3)

Delectables In The City (A Sexy Chick Lit Series)
The Fifty-Two Week Chronicles (Book 1)
Coming January 2021
A Cupcake and A Gentleman (Book 2)

My Fake Fiancé (A Sexy Rom-Com Series)
My Fake Billionaire Fiancé
Coming 2021
My Fake Celebrity Fiancé
My Fake Wedding Date Fiancé
My Fake College Professor Fiancé

CONFESSIONS OF A BOOKAHOLIC

JOSLYN WESTBROOK

BLURB

What happens when a book blogger accidentally publishes her digital diary online?

A viral *shitstorm*, that's what.

No way did I want thousands of subscribers to read my confessions—yet, that's precisely what went down last night after four too many Cosmos with my girls.

Now, Damage Control is my new middle name because my diary confessional has my roommate, Lucas Stone, written all over it.

Literally.

I've been in love with him forever—well, ever since I saw him sprint across campus naked during our first year of college.

And now that Lucas knows how I feel about him?

Well, things are destined to get awkward.

Because Lucas Stone, my BFF—the man who sleeps only one room over—just got engaged.

And his fiancée isn't me.

Confessions of a Bookaholic is a steamy, friends-to-lovers, sports romantic comedy meant for mature audiences.

INTRO

I am so fucked.

Panic swept through my veins as life took a glorious shit on me.

If one were to ask, I'd insist a laptop, desktop, cell phone —*anything digital*—come with a warning label—an informative heads-up that says in larger-than-life bold font: don't operate while sauced, you freaking idiot. Better yet, they should be equipped with a Breathalyzer that'd require one to *blow* before their liquor-steered fingers—or thumbs—graced an otherwise innocent keyboard.

Truth be told, I would have sold my soul to the devil just to get my hands on an effing time machine. One badass, fully equipped contraption that could obliterate the incidence of a mortifying online snafu.

Heart rattling, I sank into bed, its cloud-like duvet sheltering me from absolute calamity.

Breathe.

I inhaled, then glared at my phone's cracked screen, groggy eyes contemplating whether or not it was all real, a prank, or some kooky-as-fuck nightmare.

How did this even happen?

Oh, wait.

That's right.

I was tipsy.

Okay, make that shit-faced.

Liquored up.

Three sheets to the flipping wind.

And instead of drunk dialing or drunk texting, my over-achieving ass did something worse.

Drunk. *Blogging*.

Perhaps I should take you back to the sequence of events that led to *bloggergate*?

Fine. Here we go.

My name is Macy Sinclair.

I'm a UCLA graduate and former content creator for a popular book-review blog called *Confessions of a Bookaholic*. The blog was my creation. My passion. I mean, reading had always provided me a literary getaway, and writing reviews about fictional escapes was the cherry on top. *Confessions of a Bookaholic* started out minuscule, a mere pastime between coursework with only a few hundred followers. By year three in college, the blog's audience blossomed to over three-hundred thousand.

Authors. Publishing houses. Other bloggers. Booksta-grammers.

Anyone in need of a snarky, honest, no-holds-barred bookish review. I was the novel-obsessed world's version of *Gossip Girl*. Heck, the blog even had an app—a subscriber's instant notif-ication of a posted review. *Ping*.

For five years, life—along with that stupid blog—was my bitch, up until the moment said life spoon-fed me an unpleasant taste of the fuckening.

You see, three days before bloggergate, Lucas Stone—my roommate, guy bestie since forever, hunkiest member of the opposite sex to grace UCLA's football field—announced he was getting married.

Married.

Like a sonic boom, the thunder of my heart exploding was likely heard—*maybe even felt*—across the globe.

I fell apart. Crashed into a sea of despair, sinking to the bottom of its murky, tear-filled abyss.

Why? Because that was the day I'd planned to let Lucas know I was hopelessly in love with him...

ACT ONE

"If two hearts are destined together, love isn't going anywhere."

LUCAS

O*ff. Limits.*
Those two words had pretty much been the ever-lasting definition of my relationship with Macy Sinclair, my hot-as-all-fucking-hell roommate and best friend.

We'd known each other since first grade. Went to the same schools. Were neighbors. I mean, Macy was *literally* the girl next door. Through those formative years, we'd grown inseparable, and while in middle school, the two of us made a pinky-swear pact that our status would forever and always be best friends.

By our first year of high school, I wanted nothing more than to kick that dumbass pact in the balls. I'd found myself catching feelings for Macy, learning it was difficult to resist that snarky charisma, flawless face, brilliant smile, lucid-blue eyes, and her impeccably round ass. Clueless me had no idea she'd done the same—developed feelings for me stretching beyond the ties that bound our friendship. Had I taken notice, watched for subtle hints, glances, *any* kind of dead giveaway, God knows I would have done this shit differently.

Fuck. Fuck. Fuck. Me.

The emphatically correct procession of F-bombs summed up every single emotion coursing through my veins.

Shock? Elation? Bitterness? Regret?

I'd just proposed to my girlfriend with ambitious plans to tie the knot six months later, mere weeks before the long-awaited NFL draft. Life, as I saw it, was mapped out. Get married, then get scooped up by one of thirty-two pro-football teams.

Things were decent. Un-freaking-eventful.

Then...*wham!*

An out-of-nowhere, presumably unintentional, *Dear Diary* entry posted on Macy's book blog. A life-shaking notification sent to my phone via the *Confessions of a Bookaholic* phone app. I'd made it a habit of reading every damn one of her entries.

Calm. Down.

I wasn't some jock who happened to be an avid reader of romance novels and reviews on the down low. No, I read Macy's posts because I'd felt obligated, knowing the hours she'd dedicated to reading romance novels and publishing reviews. I was proud of how she'd turned a hobby into something substantial and meaningful. Still, nothing could have prepared my eyes and heart for what she'd distributed to her herd of followers that night.

DEAR DIARY,

So it's been said...when you write, sorrows disappear.

With that in mind, tonight marks my first digital diary entry. I can only hope what I'm about to write sheds this pent-up wretchedness, for I truly need to move the fuck on.

"Unrequited Love" should be the title of this inaugural entry because that, dear digital diary, is the sad and true story of my life. Which is probably why I'm such a voracious bookworm of any happily-ever-

after. I've existed vicariously through the amorous lives of book heroines, imagining I were them, and their spellbinding heroes—alpha, broody, however—were all...

Him.

Real-life confessions: For nearly five years, I've been in love with my roommate, Lucas Stone, the drool-worthy morsel of hunky-hotness who's been my best friend since forever. On top of that, I've shamefully compared past boyfriends, lovers, one-night stands, book boyfriends, and the good-looking barista at the coffee shop to Lucas. Even worse, I've entertained thoughts of his glorious face, abs, and cock while spending quality time with Mr. Stone, my trusty vibrator. Yet, foolish me has been too much of a chicken ass to divulge my true feelings.

Doesn't really matter now. Lucas is getting hitched.

I should be delighted he's happy.

Really.

I mean, everyone deserves to chase, then live out, their blissfully-ever-after. Even so, my heart's scorned. Bitter as all freaking fuck. And I've mentally kicked my own rump one thousand and one times for not fessing up and for instead forgoing divulgence. Maybe, just maybe, if I'd shared this adoration, I'd be the one Lucas plans to walk down the aisle with.

Instead, he put a ring on her finger.

Harper Kingston. Ugh.

All right, scratch the, "ugh."

Truth is, she's perfect for him. The polar opposite of me. Curly, saffron hair to my bone-straight blond. Sea-green eyes to my sky blues. A tall, slim, flawless-bodied Barbie Girl, while I'm more of a petite, snack-loving Carbie Girl. In fact, I'm actually munching on my favorite chips as I type this.

Anyway, three days ago, Lucas sailed into our house, that curved-up, hard-to-get-over smile stretched across his face. It was our friend-anniversary. A day we'd celebrated for well over fifteen years. I'd cooked *us a surprise dinner, poured our favorite white wine, and prepared to finally spill the tea, profess all my sheltered feelings. Only, before we even sat down to devour our meal, Lucas blurted, "I'm getting married! I asked Harper to marry me today."*

All I could do was nod and smile, tears—he likely assumed existed because I was elated to hear his news—pooled in my eyes. We sat at our round dining room table, the one we'd purchased at a flea market when we first moved in together, then enjoyed dinner while Lucas spoke of his and Harper's plans for the future.

Their future.

After we ate, I lied and told Lucas I had an upcoming exam to cram for. Dejected, I spent the rest of the night curled up in bed, lost in the pages of Jane Austen's Persuasion. *Turns out Anne Elliot's my spirit animal. I too am in love with someone who shall never be mine...*

I'D PROBABLY READ that blog entry five times, heart beating—*slamming*—against my ears, chest, and head, disbelief rendering me downright stupid.

Macy was in love with *me*, the newly engaged asshat.

Wedged between a boulder and a hard place, I had to act fast. As a quarterback for the Bruins, making decisions on the fly happened to be par for the course. Something practiced and learned each second the palms of my hands cradled the pigskin.

So, what did I decide to do?

Leave.

Keep my distance from Macy until I could sort shit out.

Albert Einstein once said, a clever person solves a problem, but a wise person avoids it. At the time, I thought it wise to steer clear. Protect her feelings. Safeguard the unbreakable walls of our forever-long friendship. Pretend my eyes never absorbed a single word of those confessions and erect hours of breathing space between us while the dust settled.

Did it end up being the right decision?
Yes.
No.
Maybe?

2

MACY

I blamed my bitches.

Sage and Chloe.

The so-called besties.

Seriously. If those two hadn't convinced me a girls' night out with them was better therapy than staying home binge-watching the first season of *Dead To Me*, the epic fuckstorm of consequences that followed would not have rained down on my sorry-ass life.

Throat dry as the Sahara, I dialed Sage knowing at 5 a.m., Chloe'd be no use. The Sleeping Goddess kept her phone set to do-not-disturb mode until 9 a.m.

Sage answered on the first ring, and all I could hear was her breathe out a long, seemingly annoyed exhale.

"Are you awake?" I smacked myself on the forehead, a self-scolding for asking such a lame question. Of course, she wasn't awake. We—Sage, Chloe, and I—were all out drinking until 2 a.m. the night before—a deed they'd leveraged to make me forget the guy of my fantasies who intended to live his ever-after with someone who obviously wasn't me.

"First of all," Sage hissed. "Why the F-word are you calling me at the butt crack of dawn to ask if I'm awake? Second of all, why the H-word are you even whispering?"

She was on a potty-mouth cleanse, which meant her usual cuss-like-a-sailor flytrap had been reduced to spitting out what she called "partial placeholders," hence her fluid use of "F-word" and "H-word" in place of fuck and hell.

"I don't want him to hear me," I whisper-shouted.

"Him, *who*? Wait. A. Minute," Sage gasped. "Did you get snatched by that Uber driver last night? Chucked into the trunk of his ruby-red Fiat? See? I told Chloe we shouldn't have let you hop in his car. Dude seemed to be a bit on the cray-cray side. Crossed-eyed. Wicked grin. Missing teeth. Pretty sure he looked one hundred percent, serial killer."

Sadly, I couldn't even recall catching an Uber, everything was still a blur.

"No, I didn't get snatched by the Uber guy," I explained. "You know my walls are thin. I'm whispering because I don't want Lucas to hear me."

"Lucas? Who the S-word cares if *he* hears you? Punch him in the fucking balls for getting engaged and being all Bird Box blindfolded when it comes to how you feel about him. Darn it!" she growled. "I said the F-word."

Hand over mouth, I failed at suppressing the giggle that wiggled free. For every spoken cuss word, Sage had to perform a series of squats.

Movements, along with grunts, were heard from her end of the call as she presumably counted down each knee bend. "My butt is going to look so fabulously badass from all these freaking lower-body enhancers."

"Is the *ass* in badass considered a cuss word?" Sounds of her straining forced me to lower the volume on my phone.

"Shut the F-word up and tell me why you called. After these stupid squats, I'm going back to bed."

My snort-laugh morphed into sobs as tears trickled down my cheeks. "I-I messed up, Sage. Big time."

"Messed what up?" she asked, before muttering a sequential-squat countdown.

Explaining how I'd accidentally sent a diary entry out to thousands of followers felt surreal. Being a perfectionist, I'd always been one to double—triple—check my work. But, given I was drunker than a sailor lost in a vat of vodka, there's no telling what I did that night.

After a winded gasp, Sage went all Captain Obvious. "Can't you, like...delete it? I mean, after I've had a chance to read it, of course..."

"I need my laptop to delete it and seeing how I can't even remember where I left it last night, I'm screwed."

"Living room?"

"Checked. It's not there."

"Bathroom?"

"Not there either," I told her, hopelessly. "And before you ask, I looked in the kitchen and dining room too."

"WTF, Macy. Were you *that* effing wasted?"

Armpits practically drenched, I pinched the bridge of my nose, taking in then releasing a few deep breaths. My ticker must have decided one-hundred-fifty beats per minute was the new resting heart rate. "Apparently. Besides, you know I've always been a lightweight. Shame on you and Chloe for letting me drink—"

"Two...Freaking...Cosmos, Macy," she interrupted with an assumed eye roll. "You do realize you had only *two* drinks, right?"

Only two?

Cradling my head, I whined, "They must have been pretty potent because it feels more like four."

"Maybe it *was* four...or five? Anyway, what can I do to help?"

Typically, I never allowed anyone to touch *Confessions of a Bookaholic.* It was my baby, trusted in the hands of no one but me

—the alcohol-free version, of course. Nonetheless, desperate times called for me to reach way outside my norm. Thankfully, Sage agreed to access my blog through her computer.

"Okay, I've got it. What's your password?"

Heat slithered from my cheeks, straight up to my head, practically scorching my scalp. Given the circumstances, I was beyond embarrassed to reveal the blog's log-in credentials. "Lucas Stone."

"My goldfish could have guessed that."

Audible tapping of her fingernails drumming the keyboard, gifted my heart with enough reassurance to slow its erratic roll. Howbeit, freak-out nerves had me feeling antsy, so I got out of bed, then began to pace, bare feet sinking into the plush carpet in the center of my bedroom floor.

"Are you in yet?" I chewed my lower lip. "Scroll down to today's date and click on it."

Sage's hushed reserve rallied the stampede of my heart palpitations all over again.

"Hello?" *What the hell is she doing?* "Sage? Are you there?"

"Mmm-hmm," she singsonged nonchalantly.

God, I envied how laid-back the firecracker could be when there I was, yanking every follicle of my hair out.

I bit my nails, beats of time frozen while I waited with bated breath for her to tell me if she'd found the damn entry. "Well?" I whisper-shouted. "Did you find it or not?"

"Yep. Sure did. It says Dear Diary, Entry One."

"Okay? Can you click on the link, please?"

"Done...and I've read your post." She paused, as though the already intense moment needed a dramatic interlude. "So...Mr. *Stone*, your trusty vibrator, huh?"

"Sage!" I whisper-barked, wanting to reach through my cell phone and choke her. She had a ton of nerve teasing me at a time like this. The stress alone probably caused me to age forty years. I could feel the hair color on my dome change from vibrant blond to lowly gray. "Can you please just delete the damn thing?"

"Sure. But you really oughta see the thousands of comments. I mean, seriously. They all *love* the fact you have the hots for Lucas. Although some seem to think it's a sneak-peek excerpt of a book you're currently reading. A few are even asking about the release date for *Dear Diary Entry One,* along with the name of the author, so they can add it to their Goodreads list."

I couldn't help but snicker. My followers. They, without a doubt, were hungry book whores in constant search of their next story to gobble up. It was right on point for them to think I'd shared a sneak peek into my current read.

"Yeah. I read some of their comments before I called you. It was how I found out about the post—the pings on my phone woke me. Now, can you please hurry up and delete it before anyone shares it on Facebook and Twitter?"

"Eight thousand forty-nine."

"I'm sorry?" Her quirky ass often blurted out shit that didn't make sense to me, or anyone with a pulse. "What's that?"

"Shares, Macy," she snapped as if annoyed that *Sage* wasn't my first language. "Your diary post has that many shares already. Honestly, this could be your new thing."

Really? My new *thing*? As if all of it didn't have me dwindling inside, questioning my whole purpose in life.

"Delete it!"

3

MACY

I'd never been much of a gambler.

But the analyzer in me believed there was a better-than-average shot Lucas never caught sight of my professed love for him.

About an hour after Sage deleted bloggergate, I mustered enough courage to step out of the safety zone known as my bedroom. Sure it may have been chancy to deliberately come across Lucas so soon after the incident. Still, it had to be done in order to properly assess then control whatever damage it had caused.

I'd come up with a sensible plan. Sashay into the kitchen then casually evaluate whether or not his steely blues perused those drunken confessions. He had a morning routine. And at that specific time, I expected to find my crush perched on the counter, browsing ESPN headlines on his phone as he scarfed back a bowl of Corn Flakes, hair beautifully tousled, outfitted in nothing except PJ bottoms and that book-hero-worthy naked torso. Besides being so damn easy on the eyes, Lucas was also so damn easy to predict. I'd known the charmer since he was a kid. Witnessed him go through puberty. I knew when he was lying by the subtle shift in his scruff-dotted jaw, could determine if he was angry or annoyed via a single brow lift, even when he feigned otherwise. Point is, it felt like I knew him better than anybody.

All I needed was eye contact—a gander into his soul—to ascertain whether or not Lucas Stone had read my telltale blabber.

Rounding the hallway that led to our kitchen, something seemed way off.

The giveaway?

Silence.

Lucas almost always played music, background fluff to every and anything he did, a genre dedicated to each activity.

Take for instance mealtime—be it breakfast, lunch, or dinner —he fancied country music, his gruff voice lending a sexy twang while he hummed or sang along. During showers, Lucas's prime choice was hip-hop; his rap-star articulation bouncing off the walls had a tendency to crack me up. And while doing chores around the house, heavy metal did it for him. Amusing as hell to watch while he, without fail, amped up his air-guitar romp.

Entering the kitchen, there was nothing. No sight of Lucas atop the counter. No evidence that I somehow missed what I'd witnessed every single day for the last five years.

Instead, quiet filled the space, save for the slow-drip *plink* from the leaky faucet he should have repaired a month ago.

"Lucas?" My eyes swept the one-hundred-square-foot area, expecting he'd magically spring from a cupboard. "Are ya home?"

After no response, I padded out the kitchen before rounding our narrow hallway, fervent footsteps navigating me past a notice-ably empty bathroom to the right.

As roommates, we'd established a hard set of bylaws, some-thing to preserve a regardful, comfortable living arrangement.

First, keep the bathroom clean, its door wide open when not in use, and locked when occupied. Yes, renting a small house close to campus left us very few options like a two-bedroom bungalow equipped with only one bathroom. Don't get me started on the number of times I'd walked in on Lucas and his girthy banana-conda emerging from the shower. Believe me, a girl could only take so much man candy without giving in to hormones and jumping his bones. Ergo, those continuous encounters with him *au naturel* prompted me to add that much-needed *keep-the-bath-room-door-locked-when-occupied* rule.

Second, respect one another's personal space, which in essence meant we were to stay the fuck out of each other's bedrooms.

I'd only once violated the latter when Lucas was away on a three-day Mexican Riviera cruise with Harper. There'd been a power outage, and I needed to access the electric panel housed inside his bedroom closet, another con when renting an older bungalow in Westwood.

As I neared his room, only steps away from my own to the left, my eyes caught Lucas's door ajar, sun rays illuminating each step across the laminate floor creaking beneath my toes.

Was he still sleeping?

Highly unlikely. Lucas was one of those annoying early birds, all sexy-eyed and hunky-tailed seven days a week, no matter if he'd partied the night before. Nonetheless, I was on a mission to satisfy a mean case of curiosity.

Palming the door open, I poked my head inside for a peek, the faint smell of his cologne punching me senseless. "Lucas?"

No reply.

After I'd stepped inside, uneasiness crept over me.

I knew that I shouldn't have violated our personal space rule, but damn it...where the hell was he?

Hands on hips, I stood planted in the center of his room, sizing up the neatly made bed, tickled by how organized his space appeared compared to most guys. Don't get me wrong, I was a fanatic of fellow lovers of all things structured and methodized. But given Lucas was a typical jock, the tidiness brought his organization skills to a highly respectable level.

Taking it all in, my gaze gravitated to his nightstand, and after trekking on over, I plucked one of the two framed photos featuring us.

A soft smile stretched across my face, the photo generating a faint recollection. We were seven years old, goofing off at Funtime Pizza Palace. It was my birthday, and I distinctly remembered Lucas kicking the clown for making me cry.

"You're scaring her with your stupid, big-nosed face!" he yelled, the clown hopping around on one foot, holding his injured shin in agony. I couldn't think of a time when Lucas didn't have my back, watching out for me as if he were my appointed guard.

Snickering, I set the photo back in its place, then picked up another beside it, parking my bottom onto the edge of the bed.

A sigh escaped me, warmth coating my heart as the snapshot escorted me further down the memory expressway.

It was a photograph of us, taken three years earlier, at Lake Tahoe during a winter ski adventure with a group of friends. I'd sprained my ankle after tripping on the damn skis, minutes before we had a chance to hit the slopes. At first, I thought my clumsiness had ruined my trip—the sole purpose for being there—since I obviously couldn't ski with a messed-up ankle. Yet, while everyone else set out to conquer the powder, Lucas hung with me at the lodge.

"You'd do the same if our roles were reversed," he told me, resting my foot atop a set of stacked throw pillows. I shrugged, knowing he was right.

But that weekend our close, seemingly impenetrable bestieship, along with a juvenile pinky-swear pact we'd made when we were too young to know any better, was put to the test. It had been the first time we'd come inches, seconds away from sharing a kiss—a fleeting moment of weakness while relaxing next to a warm fire—conveniently interrupted by our friends returning from the slopes. Funny thing, Lucas and I carried on like nothing had happened, neither of us ever speaking of the incident's existence.

Resting the photo back in place, I couldn't help but wonder if those stupid confessions would end up being steamrolled into nonexistence much like that almost-kiss did.

Truth be told, I hoped to fuck bloggergate *did* end up in never-ever-happened land—if not for the sake of his newly engaged status—but for the sake of our rock-solid relationship.

Exiting his bedroom, I fished my cell phone from the front pocket-pouch of my UCLA hoodie I'd always worn around the house. Regardless of the epic shitstorm that had my stomach splintering, I felt the need to determine where Lucas went. Knowing would at least yield an understanding of his mindset —hopefully.

Did he go out for a run? To practice? Harper's?

With any of those scenarios, chances were he'd been too occupied to have read anything, much less my stupid blog post.

Careful not to nick my fingertip against its cracked screen, I swiped my phone to unlock it, making a mental note to find out how my phone ended up cracked in the first place. *No more libations for me.*

Then, I thumbed off a text message to Lucas.

Hey, where are you?

4

LUCAS

"**M**an, come on! Where the fuck is your head right now, Stone?"

My attention flicked from a text message over to AJ's huff and puff—then the *whoosh* of the ball as it sailed way over my head.

Mouth outfitted in a dickish smirk, I tried to play it off even though it didn't take a rocket scientist to figure out my head wasn't on the field. "You throw like a bitch."

"And today, *Asshole the Great*"—he swiped beads of sweat off his forehead—"you obviously catch like one."

Every baller would agree hurling trash talk on the field is a player's rite of passage. AJ and I had been known to master the art of dishing insults, at times getting downright savage. No one, except Coach K, was immune though there were times he too fell victim to the wrath of our collaborative put-downs. We'd been teammates since freshman year, bonding over the inarguable fact we were two of the best on the field—both recruited during senior year in high school. Out of the three wide receivers on the team, AJ was the one I'd inevitably launch the ball to, the player I had the strongest connection with. Together, we were a dynamic force.

The Brady and Gronk of UCLA football, scoring thirty-plus touchdown passes. Friends, bros, on and off the gridiron, it wasn't unusual for us to call each other out on our shit. And by the furrowed set of brows, the pronounced flex in his jaw, it was evident AJ planned on holding nothing back. I braced for his incoming fit.

"Dude, you show up to my door at fuckcrack in the morning, saying we should bring our asses here to practice." His hands fell to his hips and, in that moment, he resembled a disgruntled old man scolding neighborhood bullies. "Yet, you've been nothing but distracted this entire time."

He wasn't wrong.

When I left home early that morning, I thought for sure getting some practice time in with AJ would help steer my mind clear of...things—divert me from all the shit I'd fled. Time on the field, be it practice or game time, often cleared my headspace, supplied that decampment we all crave.

Not that day.

Instead, I'd been reflecting, recalling Macy's words, her personal convictions splattered over the internet like mud.

Was her proclaim-to-all an accident or intentional?

Why the hell didn't she tell *me* how she felt?

Those queries made my jaw stiffen, my discombobulated heart bleed.

And when her text message hit my phone with "Hey, where are you," I stood on the field, contemplating it, blind to the fact AJ's ball was soaring toward me—the tenth, or twentieth throw I'd failed to catch that morning.

"Sorry, man. Just got shit on the brain." I slid my cell inside my short's' pocket, choosing to ignore Macy's text. "Let's call it and go grab breakfast?"

"Pancake Shack, but only if you're buying."

Inside the car, I attempted to avoid the forthcoming inquisition by blasting Drake. But I knew it was only a matter of time before the commencement of Q&A.

AJ reached over to lower the volume, abandoning that unspoken *never touch the driver's music* rule.

"So..." He drummed his long fingers along the middle console. "What the fuck is up?"

Blunt and always straight to the point. It was a respectable attribute.

Most times.

Pondering whether or not to come clean, I said nothing. Still, there was only a matter of time before questions would stream in.

AJ scoffed, openly annoyed by my reserve. "What? You have it out with Macy?"

I snapped my head in his direction, my regard bouncing between him and the road. "Why would you assume it's *Macy* and not someone like Harper?" I felt blood in my veins simmer at his presumption, more so due to its untimely truth.

"Because...Macy..."

"Because Macy, what?" I grumbled, wondering if my question was daft since AJ eyeballed me like there were three dicks strapped to my face.

"Dude"—he shook his head, abruptly shifting his view out the passenger side window—"maybe it's time you ask yourself that question."

What. The. Fuck?

Halting at a red light, my thumbs rapped the steering wheel, its repetitive sound and motion keeping me calm, relaxed, allowing for time to breathe, to ease past the lump of irritation shearing my throat. "And by that you mean...?"

AJ shifted, plucking his cell phone from the pocket of his sweatpants. "Never mind." The three-syllabled retort was chased by an eye roll right before his finger flicked the phone screen, parading him through profiles of friends he followed on the campus app called UCChat. "None of it really fucking matters considering you chose Harper."

An intrusive *beep* from a red minivan in back of us swallowed the moment, a white-haired old lady behind the wheel fussing at me to get going.

Her feisty spirit brought out a chuckle. "Okay, lady. Thanks for letting me know the light turned green."

Gunning the accelerator, I didn't know the best way to respond to AJ's comment without sounding like a bitch. He'd never been a member of the Harper Kingston fan club. Looking back, none of my friends had been—although I never understood why.

Harper was great on paper.

Marriage material with brains, beauty, and an incredibly fierce body that launched her into a triple-threat sphere.

Plus, being Coach K's daughter—yep, the coach's daughter—meant she'd come from respectable lineage.

Harper seemed downright perfect for me, perfect for all roads paved forward.

Be it the case, why the fuck did I have a gaping hole in my chest, feeling as though my head were underwater, immersed in a sinkhole of unfathomable doubt?

Damn. Confessions.

Rolling into Pancake Shack's parking lot, I pumped my fist, relieved there wasn't the usual line of UCLA students waiting outside. The growls and rumbles coming from my gut told me, loud and clear, my stomach wasn't letting me off the hook for skipping breakfast.

Known for its signature strawberry-banana pancakes, the trendy mom-and-pop-style café was where students gathered before, after, in between, or *during* classes, catering to those hybrids who, like Macy, juggled traditional and online courses. I'd never been disciplined enough for online studies, regardless of the fact my major, Physical Education, didn't offer such an option.

Macy, on the other hand, excelled at distant learning, and since eighty percent of her classes were taken online, she loved having control over her time.

After squeezing in between a parked motorcycle to the left and a Honda to the right, I shifted my car into park.

AJ unfastened the seatbelt, still engrossed in his phone as his fingers interlocked the handle to open the door, but he paused as soon as he heard me say, "Spit out what you have against Harper." It may have been one of those questions one would later regret tossing out; nonetheless, my brain craved the response much like a pregnant woman does pickle-flavored ice cream.

Turning to face me, AJ's unconcealed perusal leveled onto mine. "She's not Macy."

5

Hours.

Not just two or three.

Five excruciating hours had gone by with no reply from Lucas. Dickhead.

Avoidance happened to be his coat of armor, a personal protection shield he brandished like Captain Freaking America.

Mr. Stone's flagrant brush-off only signified he'd read *everything*, the realization tightening my chest till normal breathing seemed too far-fetched.

Be that as it may, I surmised damage control would become this chick's obsession, as soon as a plausible course of action was laid out. Guidance from besties who specialized in clusterfuck management was a definite must.

Highly skilled in slyness, anyone would have agreed Chloe and Sage could teach a Masterclass on scheming. Convinced they'd know what to do, I headed over to their place, even though chugging cocktails with them was kind of what planted me face-first in this sticky mess to begin with.

"Want me to order us some pizza?" Chloe poured white wine into three coffee mugs lined up on the counter. "Pizza cures all."

"Uh, I beg to differ," Sage announced, helping herself to one of the mugs, her initial sip accompanied by a slurp. "Hot sex is what cures all."

"Okay, fine." Chloe reached across the counter, passing me one of the Moscato-filled mugs, pink-stained lips kicked up into a barefaced smirk. She'd been known to dish an occasional evil eye, and the glare she had fixed on Sage could cut glass on all the high rises in Dubai. "Want me to order us some *hot sex* then?"

"Would ya, hon?" Sage arched a brow, the look of sarcasm slapped on her face like a pore-cleansing facial mask. "I'll take mine meaty with extra sauce."

Kid you not, watching the two of them bounce witty comebacks back and forth was like being up close and center at a comedic stage show—A Night at the Improv with Sage and Chloe.

Chloe wrote down our picky order—one-third pineapple with light sauce, another third sausage and extra cheese, and the last portion jalapeño and chicken. When she placed the pencil onto the counter, we all watched as it rolled off and onto the floor.

Pooch, their Siamese cat, trotted in and snagged the pencil into his mouth, then ran off with it like a bat out of hell.

"Cat thinks he's a freaking dog," Sage said. "Takes off with stuff, charges out the cat door flap Chloe installed, then buries the stolen goods deep inside the courtyard flower bed." She gulped a swig of wine. "Swear to God he ran off with my vibrator the other day. Poor thing is probably six feet under, missing my vajayjay."

I shrugged. "Maybe you shouldn't have named your cat Pooch."

When the pizza arrived, the three of us settled on their living room floor, stuffing our faces, sipping wine, and of course, devising.

"I say you prance around your house naked from now on," Chloe babbled, pausing to snag a sip of wine. "Breakfast dolled up in your birthday suit. Netflix on the couch, garment free. Household chores with nothing but your glorious ass and tits on display. I mean, sooner or later, Lucas—along with his cock—will have no choice but to kick Harper to the curb and concede to your proclaimed love for him."

Sage doused her slice of pizza in ranch dressing, noggin bobbing as though what she'd just heard made sense. "That might actually work. Remember that scene in *The Breakup* when Jennifer Anniston's character strutted around their apartment bare and newly waxed? It was pleasurable torture for Vince Vaughn's character." She bit into the ranch-coated slice. "I've seen you naked, Macy. Believe me, Lucas will bust a nut once he—"

"Okay," I interjected, hands up. "You both need to shut up forever." I cracked up, done with their zany, albeit somewhat tempting, suggestion. "I will *not* prance around my house naked...yet."

Heads tossed back, we busted our guts, the swigs of sweet wine consumed making us noticeably giddy. Their company proved to be sustenance for my broken soul to thrive on, life support that kept my heart pumping when all I wanted to do was curl up in bed with a box of dark chocolates and the emotionally gritty Kennedy Fox novel on my read-and-review list.

Kidding aside, I needed a *real* plan. Cerebral. Smart. One that didn't involve dragging myself through further embarrassment.

"Come on, ladies." I reached for another slice, eschewing its high-calorie count. "Give me something more sagacious than flashing my goodies."

Brown-haired head atilt, Sage blinked twice, then snagged her cell off her lap, thumb fixed to the button that awakened the know-it-all assistant. "Siri, what the *fuck* does 'sagacious' mean?"

"Squats!" Chloe and I barked, bits of pizza spewing from our mouths.

Sage growled, hauling herself off the carpeted floor. "Stupid potty-mouth cleanse. Stupid squats. Stupid big-ass words like *sagacious* that normal people don't use."

"*Sagacious. Having or showing keen mental discernment and good judgment; wise or shrewd.*"

Our collective eyes flicked to Sage's phone facedown on the floor. We couldn't help but laugh, the delayed timing of Siri's robotic response, funny as all fucking hell.

Thirty minutes later, bellies full and achy from copious amounts of food and laughter, we lounged on the balcony that faced their charming courtyard. Fairy-light-dressed palm trees flickered bright, and the warm breeze that sashayed around us was airy enough to lull our woozy asses into a post-food-and-wine slumber.

Chloe cleared her throat, slaying any thoughts we might've been lost in. "You know, there are three letters we have yet to open. Perhaps the news each of them holds can be a deciding factor in all of this."

Always pragmatic, Chloe brought up a fair point.

Those letters. I swear, just the mere thought of them made my heart seize.

All majoring in journalism, we had a mutual love for writing, along with ambitious dreams to someday work for a prestigious magazine. During the summer semester, Professor Mays suggested we apply for a winter internship with *Hot Shot* magazine, and for shits and giggles, we did, amused by the possibility. The letters of acceptance—*or probably rejection*—landed in our mailboxes two days ago and remained unopened, the unknown far less nerve-wracking than the known. We'd vowed to keep each personal letter housed in our purses ready to open, together, whenever we grew some damn balls.

If accepted, the three-month internship would take one, or hopefully all of us to New York City, which was doable since eighty percent of our classes were already online. However, rejection and acceptance seemed equally terrifying. We found ourselves hiding from either possibility like apocalypse survivors hide from the undead.

"I say we go ahead and open those flipping envelopes," Chloe told us, her emerald-greens twinkling as bright as the lights on their courtyard. "We've held out long enough, not to mention acceptance comes with a deadline to respond."

"Yep," Sage agreed. "Imagine if we're accepted? Oh, the freaking joy!" She rose to her feet, arms fanned out, ebony locks fluttering as she twirled around the small balcony. "Macy can tell Lucas, that clueless motherhumper, to eff off as she sails toward New York."

Thoughts of a possible getaway soothed me, its timely convenience essential in order to flee the mishmash my drunk ass and my intoxicated heart produced with one measly click. God knows the last thing I wanted was to build a block of emotions between Lucas and Harper, nor a wall of awkwardness between me and the guy who'd been my best friend since the time other boys our age gave me hives.

Stomach flip-flopping, I nodded, unable to fight the resolved smirk pulling at my lips. "It's settled, ladies. There's unopened mail we must tend to."

6

LUCAS

Truth.

It's what AJ served hot and ready like the glazed donuts we sometimes picked up on our way to early morning football practices. Truth is what one avoids when trying to keep emotions in check, afraid of facing its ensuing consequences.

She's not Macy.

AJ could've just stopped right there because those three words alone rode me hard. No one compared to Macy, a ball-busting factoid better known as my *hidden* truth.

Feigning confusion I asked, "What's that supposed to mean?" I stroked the scruff on my jaw, aware my question would go down as the second stupidest one I'd asked all year—the first stupidest one had oozed out of my mouth like Nickelodeon slime days before. I knew what AJ had meant, yet my bullheaded ass preferred to hear it out loud from a voice other than the one buzzing in my head.

"Seriously, bro? You really need to ask?" He settled back into the passenger seat as though gearing up for some Dr. Phil heart-to-heart. "She's made for you. Don't get me wrong, Harper's definitely got it goin' on. Cute, dope body...yadda yadda yadda. But everyone except you"—he punched my shoulder—"can see your whole demeanor shift whenever Macy's around. You actually glow like that effing vampire pretty boy in Twilight." He removed his ball cap to scratch his head, then slapped it back into place. "What more can I say, man? You pulled a shock-and-awe by proposing to Harper and I kicked myself for not opening my mouth about it before, telling you what a dumb-ass you were for hooking up with someone like Harper instead of Macy. I mean, she's not your *person,* your ride or die. Plus, most times, she acts like a stuck-up B."

He stalled for a few beats as though waiting for me to react to his last comment. There was no need; Harper had a propensity to be a conceited little bitch—a shortcoming I guess only I'd learned to tolerate over time.

At my blatant nonreaction, he went on. "Truthfully, we all expected you'd end up with Macy. Especially considering you've made it perfectly clear *none* of us can fucking touch her—well, not me since, you know...Sage."

AJ and Sage. Two destined lovers who'd yet to figure shit out. Their on-and-off relationship gave me whiplash. Which made me ponder whether or not I should've had my ears open to meant-for-you insight from someone who, like me, failed to grasp a bona-fide clue. While on my soapbox, I will unashamedly admit I did warn my teammates to steer clear of Macy. If I couldn't have her—no thanks to that stupid "friends only" pact—damn straight none of those fuckers could either.

Listening to AJ spit nothing but facts made the gaping hole in my chest grow tenfold.

After our powwow, we decided to grab Pancake Shack's special to go. When I dropped AJ off at his house, it felt way too soon to head back home—and showing up to Harper's seemed out of place until I got my mind straight.

Instead, I trekked over to more neutral territory.

"WELL, look at what the old pussy cat dragged in. I just mentioned to your dad that we'd probably see you today." Mom smiled up at me, standing on her tiptoes, enveloping me in a hug before I even made it through the threshold. She cupped my face in her hands. "Interesting read, that Bookaholic post, huh?"

I breathed, shifting my gaze downward, quick to avoid Mom's astute one. I figured she'd eyed the post, a super fangirl of Macy since...always.

Trailing her, I kicked the door shut behind us, then beelined straight for the kitchen. The yumminess in the bag of Pancake Shack grub I held—pancakes, bacon, scrambled eggs—taunted my nostrils, screaming to be devoured.

Lola and Jack, two Pomeranian mega-brats, barreled at me, yapping, nipping at my ankles as I lugged along. Without fail, each time I walked through the door, those two attacked me, tails wagging as though they hadn't seen me since the Earth's last orbit around the Sun.

"Now, now. Calm down, you crazy kids. Let your brother settle in," Mom cooed, peeling my furry-sibling appendages off me.

The home in Beverly Hills—all six thousand square feet of it —had always been my go-to spot, popping in for unannounced visits twice, sometimes three times a week. I was lucky to have a rock-solid relationship with my parents even when I made choices they didn't agree with.

Inside the spacious kitchen, Dad stood loading the dishwasher with what appeared to be their own breakfast cups and plates. "Son," he said with a nod. "You ready for Saturday's big game? Those Ducks are looking pretty fierce now that they've got Sherlock as a QB. Rumor has it they're in town early, using SC's field for practice."

My father, the distinguished older version of me, held a gleam in his eyes, bright enough to illuminate Alaska's darkest nights. Mr. Football Obsessed had the gridiron seared into his brain. Discussions about football brought him a sense of pride and mirth—though who could blame his obsession? An ex-pro player, Dad would no doubt live and breathe the game forever, times infinity.

"Yep, we've reviewed past game footage, studied their formations," I told him, plopping onto one of the bar stools lined up at the center island. "They're good, but not good enough to cause concern."

It's not that I meant to sound cocky. With our talent, truth was the Bruin's reign had been on an unstoppable winning streak. Besides that, we knew we had to win the homecoming game against the Ducks. Their newly acquired quarterback, Sherlock Benson, was a prick who used to lead our rivals at SC. The fuckass played like a dick, and always tossed out filthy trash talk about how he banged my girl right before the game.

Mom offered me a cup of coffee, then hauled her petite self onto the stool to the right of mine, feet dangling inches above the ground.

"So," she singsonged, flipping through pages of People magazine. "Anything on your mind?"

There was no need to tear my gaze from the container of chow to see she had her perceptive glare nailed to me. As a psychologist, Mom couldn't ignore her predisposition to survey, analyze, and diagnose.

"I've always got something on my mind." I took a bite of crispy bacon, fighting off the intrepid smirk playing on my mouth.

"Where's your other half?" Dad's tenor butted in as he nudged the dishwasher door closed.

"Oh, I haven't seen Harper since—"

"I meant Macy, Son. You never show up here without her."

Was it fuck-me day?

Because every minute of it had been chock-full of Macy truths stabbing me in my gut like daggers. *Yes*, we'd often made our visits back home together, first to her parents' house next door, then mine, and vice versa. But, shit, not always.

Taking a sip of coffee, I rolled my eyes. "We're not joined at the hip, Dad."

I watched Herculean Mr. Stone mosey on over to the center island, stride omnipotent and effortless. As he eased onto the stool to my left, it didn't go unnoticed how he, and that football-beefy stature, towered over me even while seated.

I gulped.

Pretty sure being sandwiched between a pair of all-knowing parents was worse than undergoing a Law & Order-style interrogation.

"We can skip the bullshit chatter and discuss those confessions Macy spilled all over the internet this morning."

Shock slithered to the base of my throat, its viscosity thicker than mud coasting downhill in a storm. Mom didn't even bother tiptoeing around the big-ass elephant consuming the room, consuming my life.

Internally, I scoffed.

Wasn't this supposed to be a venture into neutral territory?

The mental pop quiz stumped me, multiple-choice answers coming at me in spades.

A: Yep.

B: Nope.

C: Sometimes.

D: All of the above.

Perhaps Macy Sinclair would never be neutral territory amongst those in my circle.

Guard up, I flicked my view to the petite spitfire beside me, frustration riding the puff of air I blew out. "Mom, I didn't come here to talk about Macy."

Arms folded, she tipped her chin up defiantly. "How about we talk about Harper Kingston instead?"

7

LUCAS

"She's inside the pool house, *Señor* Stone." Standing in the foyer, fingers gripped to a tray bearing Caesar salad, a grilled cheese sandwich, and *expensive* bottled water, Coach K's housekeeper, Valentina, smiled bashfully. "I'll go with you? *Señorita* Kingston's only expecting this snack. I don't think she's ready for visitors."

Still residing with her parents—Sean Kingston, *Coach K* of UCLA Bruins Football, and Leyla Diamond-Kingston of *Diamond Bottled Water,* heiress to the aforementioned *expensive* water—Harper pretty much lived the life of a socialite. She didn't attend college, she dropped out of UCLA shortly after we got serious. She also didn't have a job; well, not unless being the face of Diamond Bottled Water could be considered a job. Given she'd earned a fuckwad of dough for each photo snapped, showcasing her sipping from overpriced diamond-embossed bottles, perhaps something of its stature could've been considered a job. Still, Harper had a knack for Computer Science, and, as such, I expected the computer brainiac to attain a degree and end up working for some Fortune 500 as a pro hacker or something. I'll admit being a tad put-off when she mentioned she didn't need a degree or a career—my affinity toward career-driven women undoubtedly strong. "I've got Diamond Water and a guy who's gonna make millions in the NFL," is what she'd once told me without a hint of hesitation.

Valentina scurried toward the pool house, me stalking behind, the squeaks of my sneakers echoing as we crossed the marble-floored space. The Bel Air home, with its moneyed and pretentious decor, must have been ten times the size of the twelve-hundred-square-foot bungalow I shared with Macy.

Macy. A fleeting, unexpected quiver in my heart caused me to stumble. Macy was what made me decide to stop by Harper's before going home, especially after the kick-in-the-ass boost from Mom and Dad.

"Careful, *Señor* Stone," Valentina cautioned over her shoulder. "The floor is real slippery from an early morning wax."

Rap music blared as we neared the mostly-glass pool house where Harper could be seen waving a set of poms-poms, laughing and *twerking,* wearing nothing but a fluorescent-orange string bikini.

Admittedly, her slim curves, scarlet hair, and pretty face were easy on the eyes. Plus that heart-shaped, always-painted-red mouth got fucked by my cock—never at my house, Macy and I had agreed to have no overnight guests—on the regular. Nothing except pure, unadulterated oral ever occurred between us, not that the act of giving head is *pure* and *unadulterated.* It takes an experienced, naughty mouth to blow a dude's gasket. Yet, Harper Kingston claimed to be a virgin who wanted to wait until marriage before "intercourse"—her pubescent word choice, not mine. Rumors about her sexual appetite smeared doubts in my head about her virginity. Regardless, I continued on with our relationship all the way to the point where idiotic me asked for her hand in marriage—which, by the way, was the first stupidest question I'd asked all year.

Is Harper the woman of your dreams, or the woman you've settled for because you believe the woman of your dreams is completely off-limits?

It's the question my mother pitched, the kickoff to our candid, eye-opening discussion about Harper and my pent-up feelings toward my childhood friend.

Truth of the matter—as AJ declared—Harper wasn't Macy.

Neither was Julia, Lori, Skye, or any other girlfriends and one-nighters of my past. In fact, every single one turned out to be the exact opposite of Macy, not only by way of looks, but also personality. None were blond. None had blue eyes. All were tall and slim, instead of petite with curves in all the best places. Moreover, not a single one possessed the sarcastic mouth, the sharp wit that made my dick twitch.

I'd avoided anyone who might remind me of Macy, subconsciously choosing women less like my *type*, knowing damn well it wouldn't work out between us, since my heart craved someone else.

Mom's psychological pull saved me from careening headfirst into what could have easily been a living hell. Her thought-provoking pep talk—triggered by Macy's confessions—helped me pivot, make a cognitive choice to cross the line of scrimmage that would allow me and my best friend to take our years-long friendship to another level.

As soon as I ended things with Harper.

"*Señorita* Kingston is not expecting you, right?" Valentina spun around to face me, her half smile a veil to her flustered nerves.

"Nope." My one-worded ejection probably seemed curt. But it pissed me off that even though we'd been together three years, Harper preferred a heads-up before I stopped by. A text. Phone call. Prearranged suck-me date.

Valentina paused near the massive-sized swimming pool about twenty feet from the sliding doors that gave entry to the pool house. "She already has a friend over. Maybe you should wait here by the pool while I go get her?"

Harper's giggles grew louder as she pranced, ass bouncing to shit I'd never heard before. The pom-poms she waved like a *Bring it On* reject collapsed to the floor. Then, in almost slow motion, she twirled around, pulling her bikini top string loose before the near-nothing piece of fabric floated to the floor leaving her tits on full display.

"Nah, I'd much rather surprise her," is what I told Valentina, shouldering past the stubby little housekeeper and her wide-open mouth. I tromped toward the pool house, heartbeat kicked up a notch, wondering what the actual fuck Harper was doing.

"But, *Señor* Stone," Valentina called out, padding after me. "Maybe she's a little busy right now."

When I slid the glass doors open, Harper whirled around with a screeching gasp, all jaw-dropped, palms over her chest, doing their best to shield her surgically-enhanced rack.

My narrowed glare flicked from a crimson-faced, stupefied Harper onto something—*someone*—I least expected.

Sprawled out on the couch was Sherlock Benson—rival, trash-talking quarterback from hell—wearing nothing but a pillow over his junk and that fucking asshole smirk he brandished out on the field. "Uh, this is awkward," he said, sounding like a douche with a stupid-ass name.

"No shit, Sherlock." If I had any fucks to give, I would've punched him in the throat *and* the balls. Yet some blessings come in the ugliest of disguises.

Fist over mouth, I chuckled.

Guffawed.

Laughed my ass off as though my mind was lost, tempted to stop and pinch myself because none of it seemed real.

None. Of. It.

Including the blog post I'd read earlier that morning.

Valentina stumbled in, huffing and puffing, apologizing to her half-naked boss for the intrusion. "*Señorita*"—she set the tray of food onto a side table beside the sliding doors—"I tried to make him wait outside."

Like a Mirandized criminal, Harper remained silent as she scooped up her bikini top, evidently too frazzled to put it back on without a struggle. My eyes glazed over the screwed-up face of the woman I was dumb enough to propose to, disgust streaming through the blood pumping oxygen to my brain. Harper Kingston turned out to be a cheating slut, with a team rival, her *father's* rival, no less.

Given the timely circumstances, that let-her-down-easy breakup spiel I'd practiced during the forty-minute drive over from my parents' house seemed needless, out of context, and plain stupid.

Instead, I went for a less-is-more approach, deciding three succinct words would more than suffice.

"We're fucking done."

8

Hey, I'm home. Can we talk?

Mr. Evasive's text message lit up my cell shortly after 8 p.m., right as my head hit the pillow. Anytime before midnight would have normally been considered too early of a bedtime for me. After-dark hours were dedicated to online coursework, and since I had a sociology paper due, my ass should have been sitting at our kitchen table, energy drink and carb-filled snacks at the ready. Given the day's events, however, sleep beckoned with a demand for me to squeeze my eyes shut and dream the world's biggest shitstorm day away. Besides, in order to complete online assignments, I needed my stupid laptop, and that dirty little accomplice to bloggergate had yet to be found.

Grimacing, I eyed his tardy text, contemplating whether or not to ignore it, just as I'd ignored the patter of his footsteps meandering past my bedroom door when he arrived home twenty minutes earlier.

To be honest, I'd grown downright irritated with Lucas Stone. I mean, what kind of a best friend allowed twelve hours to saunter by before he finally responded to a text with some breezy, non-fucking-chalant "Hey, I'm home. Can we talk?" bullshit?

Blood simmering, I fired off a quick reply.

Me: No.

Good one, right? One-hundred percent straight and to the point.

Text bubbles bounced on the screen, my heart thumping in anticipation.

Lucas: Why not?

Seriously, dude?

Thumbs pounding the cracked screen, I keyed in my response.

Me: Because you're a duck.

Seconds later, Lucas deployed an army of duck emojis to my phone.

Ugh. I swear, autocorrect had a personal vendetta against me.

Me: DUCK! I meant to type, you're a duck!

This time my smart-ass roombestie replied with a Donald Duck GIF. There was no use trying to quell the snicker that slipped free; shit was hilarious.

Beats skedaddled by before another message came through.

Lucas: Hey, I'm sorry. I should've replied to your text earlier, should've had the decency not to leave you hanging.

Tears pricked my eyes, a fury of the day's emotional roller coaster coursing through me. He was trying to butter me up and, dammit, I hated how easily it worked.

Me: Fine. Apology accepted. But I'm not quite ready to talk.

The half-truth set my belly ablaze. Part of me wanted to talk, longed to get everything officially out in the open, evaporate the cloud of awkwardness destined to linger over us forevermore.

Lucas: No talking. Just ice cream. I picked up a gallon of our favorite from CreamWorks.

Me: Mocha Mania?

Lucas: You know it. Meet me in the kitchen in five? I need to start a load of laundry first.

He knew I'd cave, clever to coax me with my favorite ice cream as though I were Eve, unable to resist forbidden fruit.

Me: Okay, but you're still a duck.

Of course, I typed duck instead of dick on purpose, knowing damn well he'd have some smart-ass reply.

Lucas: Quack, quack.

Jerk.

Inside the kitchen, Lucas had his head in the fridge, tightly corded muscles along his back taunting me through his T-shirt. Also taunting me was a gallon of CreamWorks Mocha Mania on the table beside two plastic spoons, a pile of napkins, and my missing laptop.

"Has this laptop been here the whole time? I could've sworn the kitchen was the first place I searched."

Lucas spun around to face me, armed with a can of whipped cream, and a turned-up mouth that could beguile bras and panties off a group of cloistered nuns. Tall, at least six-foot-two to my five-foot-three, dark and beyond yummy, he'd always been desirable, and similar to times before, one glance at his beautiful, triangular visage, those narcotic moon-blues—which were coequally responsible for some of my most indecent fantasies—there I was willing my stubborn heart to refrain from having a full-blown swoon attack.

"Nope." The clarification flowed out of his mouth bedazzled with a smirk. "I found your laptop in the laundry room next to an empty wineglass on top of the dryer." Typically, Lucas had an authoritative voice that commanded attention. Yet, in that instance his timbre sounded smooth, chill enough to chase away the day's worries, like a night at the beach illuminated by a crescent moon and a thousand stars.

Practically mush, I pulled out a chair, then eased onto it, freeing my gaze from the man who made my whole body flutter.

"Laundry room? Wineglass?" I bobbed my head, coming to

terms with how and where bloggergate was conceived. "Can't remember taking it into the laundry room, much less pouring myself a glass of wine." I removed the lid off the gallon of ice cream, the aroma of mocha flirting with my nose. "Pretty sure drinking a glass of wine after chugging Cosmos goes against all FDA warning labels."

Lucas closed the fridge, then took two, long-legged strides over to the table, setting the can of whipped cream beside the ice cream. "Cosmos, huh?" He plopped onto the chair beside me, his knee brushing against mine. "Sounds a bit too Sex and the Cityish for you."

Ignoring the fact it only took an innocent Lucas Stone knee brush to make my breath hitch, I smiled calmly then said, "Sage and Chloe's idea."

Lucas chuckled as he plucked the whipped cream off the table, shaking the can as if he were a bartender mixing a drink. Flicking the lid off, he dipped the can, then squirted dollops of velvety goodness on top of the ice cream before setting the can back down. Handing me a plastic spoon, he flashed a semi-wicked grin. "Before we obliterate Mocha Mania, let's go over the rules."

I snatched the spoon out of his hand, eyes rolling because with Lucas there were always nitwitted rules to games he made up on the fly. "Wow, *obliterate*?" I raised a mocking brow. "Such a smart word for an ass." I dipped my spoon in a cloud of whipped cream, retrieving it to my mouth for a taste.

"Well, they don't call me *a smart-ass* for nothin'."

Banter Camp. Seriously, it's what I signed up for when I decided to live with Lucas. "Shut up and bark out the rules."

"All right," he said, shifting in his seat, the adjustment stealing his knee from mine. But, as if he too craved the reconnection, Lucas shifted back, giving us that subtle yet satisfying contact once more. "I may have agreed to no talking in my text message, but how about for every five spoonfuls of ice cream consumed, we spit out one word that describes how we're feeling right now."

I blinked, weighing whether or not a gallon of Mocha Mania was really worth it. Lucas loved mind-analysis games, likely picking up the trait from his psychologist mother. "Fine. But absolutely no elaborating," I insisted, eyes narrowed, spoon pointed in his direction. "No trying to get me to add more details to accompany any of my one-word descriptions."

We savored our first spoonfuls of sinfully good ice cream in silence, and once Lucas finished his fifth bite, he kicked off the shenanigans. "Optimistic."

I swallowed, then begrudgingly offered my first contribution to the word-game madness. "Embarrassed."

We ate more Mocha Mania, our spoons colliding at every dip back into the tub of too-good-to-be-real indulgence.

"Content," Lucas said without a flinch.

"Moronic."

Minutes later, Lucas unleashed his next word, husky and soft. "Relieved."

My eyes flitted to his, ecstatic butterflies dancing around my heart as our gazes swam in a sea of intoxicating emotions.

Of all the descriptive words in the English language, *optimistic, content,* and *relieved* weren't any I'd expected him to choose. Flabbergasted, disturbed, humiliated—now those were words, *feelings,* I figured he'd serve stone-faced and unimpressed.

Confused by the heady look in his electric blues, the undeniable heat swirling between us, I yanked my gaze away from his, too afraid of what seemed inevitable.

"Macy," he murmured, commanding my chin up with the tip of his index finger. "Look at me."

Oh, how difficult it was to defy the appeal as he inched closer, his chair scraping the linoleum beneath it.

The delicious way he smelled didn't help—a concoction of

Lucas, fabric softener, and mocha from ice cream that had paved the way to this moment. One inch more and we would have been a hair's breadth apart, our lips coming together in a kiss surpassing those imagined in my wettest dreams.

Still, no matter how much I wanted, *ached* to feel his full lips pressed to mine, become unraveled in those burly, powerhouse arms, Lucas Stone was involved with a woman I would never measure up to. She had beauty, brains, and most of all, his heart. Harper seemed like a real catch, while I was merely a catch and release.

Panic-stricken, I got to my feet, head shaking as I fled to my bedroom, unwilling to take part in something we'd both regret.

The sound of Lucas's footsteps masked the drum of my heartbeat as he trailed behind me, and when I reached my bedroom door, he grabbed hold of my elbow, spinning me around to face him.

"Macy, wait." He killed any space left between us, my back rigid against the bedroom door, the pad of his thumb soft against my cheek. "I need to tell you something."

I didn't want to hear it, didn't want to barrel down a road that would lead to absolute devastation—for Harper, for me, for all three of us.

Before he could utter another word, I spoke first, revealing a temporary antidote to bloggergate blues. "I'm leaving for New York in two days."

9

LUCAS

"So, you let her go?" AJ tossed his towel into the tattered, blue-and-gold gym bag he'd had since freshman year. It's not like he didn't have a new one, but that tired old thing, dubbed his lucky bag, got its use the week before any big game.

We were just four days away from our game against the Ducks and had spent an entire two-hour practice leveling up our offensive plays. Oregon had a tight offensive line, and Coach K wanted to make damn sure we didn't hand them our asses while on our home turf.

Exhausted, I didn't particularly care to have a conversation that would drag me back to two nights ago—when Macy's announcement felt more jarring than two swift kicks in the nuts.

"What do you mean, *let her go*?" I chased a jeer-laced chuckle away with a scoff. "Like Macy needed my permission?"

He flashed a look, shouldering the UCLA locker room doors open, a colder-than-seasonably-normal gust striking us like a monster truck. "Come on, don't dick around. I meant you let her go all the way to New York with stuff between the two of you left in limbo? You should have at least told her you ended shit with Harper before she left."

Here we go, another episode of the Advice From AJ show.

"Dude, stop." I followed him through the open doors. "Macy's only gonna be in New York for a week. I'll tell her all about my slutty ex when she gets back."

News about my breakup could wait. The last thing I wanted was to bomb Macy's mind space, steal the focus from what mattered. She couldn't pass up the chance to partake in a week's long interview for a winter internship at *Hot Shot*. Working for a mainstream magazine had been Macy's lifelong dream, much like playing pro-football was mine. An opportunity like that didn't come around more than once. She needed to go—I needed to *let her go*—regardless of how much the timing sucked. Her attention had to be one-hundred percent focused.

AJ shook his head as he walked alongside me to the parking lot. "Whatevs, man, do what you want. *Don't* take my advice." He slung the raggedy bag over his shoulder. "But, I think you're making a huge mistake."

I rolled my eyes, irritated that a guy who wouldn't know advice if it bit him in the dick dished it out like Dear Abby.

Deflecting, I asked, "What about Sage? You let her go all the way to New York single?"

"Hell, no. We got back together two days ago."

I snickered, feeling the least bit shocked. "Of course you did."

Once we reached our cars, we spoke about the upcoming game and a History assignment he forgot was due the next day, then we did our bro handshake before slipping into our rides and driving off.

At home, the place seemed eerily quiet with Macy gone. I missed her gorgeous, always-smiling face, hearing her hiccup after a fit of laughter, and even the mess she'd leave on the kitchen counter after preparing us an impromptu meal.

Although admitting so made me heave, AJ couldn't have been more right. I should've told Macy what went down with Harper.

Likewise, maybe I shouldn't have allowed her to leave without divulging my feelings, without coming clean about how I'd spent years reprimanding my cock for reacting to the sound of her voice, without telling her those confessions mirrored my own sentiments. Yet, that face-slapping news she spat out shook me, turning a moment destined to be our first lip-and-tongue soiree into nothing more than talk about her once-in-a-lifetime interview. Days that followed were spent helping her get packed and organized for the last-minute trip—which included a first-class plane ticket and a suite at the acclaimed Plaza Hotel—all funded by the popular magazine. *Hot Shot's* offer had almost expired, and according to Macy, the team of recruiters was eager to have Sage, Chloe, and her join the rest of the group of potential interns at the week-long event.

After a shower, I slipped into sweatpants, ordered pizza, then scrolled through the UCChat app, my lips curving up when I spotted a pic that Macy posted featuring her, Sage, and Chloe in front of their Times Square hotel.

Rosy cheeks, shopping bags in hand, she looked happy, unfazed by the fact that just two nights ago, when we sat beside each other, knees grazing, erratic heartbeats swirling between us, the unfinished moment cast yet another cloud of awkwardness over our friendship.

Like a swarm of bats in a cave, the rush of *what-ifs* filled my mind. What if she didn't freak out and run toward her room? What if my mouth tasted hers? What if years ago I admitted my feelings were so much more than best friends? What if I wasn't a dickhead who chased other girls when the one I truly desired was right here with me?

Fuck me, fuck this shit, I grimaced internally.

Eyeing the time on my phone, the numbers displayed 4 p.m. —*7 p.m. in New York*—which told me it wasn't too late to call someone who had an early morning interview. I exited the social app, my thumb hovering over Macy's number when her name flashed on the screen.

"Hey, I just saw your pic on UCChat and was literally about to call you right now." I smiled, cognizant of the fact our minds must have crossed paths.

"Well, it's not like we've never been accused of being the same person."

The mischief in her voice was refreshing, enabling me to picture that bow-shaped mouth kicked up in a coquettish smirk, powerful enough to liquefy the sun.

"Are you ready for tomorrow's interview?" My question served as an ice breaker and something to quench curiosity.

"Yeah, but honestly, I've no idea what to expect, which makes me wanna poke my eyes out and puke."

"What can I do to help?"

"You know what? Hearing your voice is already helping."

Since we'd done nothing more than text since she landed and checked into her hotel, we caught up, chatting about their fancy suite and stuff she, Sage, and Chloe had done so far in the Big Apple.

Shopping. Sightseeing. Pizza.

"Speaking of Pizza, I just ordered some, though nothing can top New York pizza."

"Don't forget the bagels and cheesecake. I mean, New York should probably own the rights to pizza, bagels, cheesecake, and ballsy jaywalkers." She laughed softly at her own words, and I swear the sound of those giggles made my cock jump.

Silence pulsed by, both presumably swept away in our own thoughts. Personally, I got lost conjuring up ways to open up dialogue, lead us back to the other night when I wanted to spill how I'd broken up with Harper, admit that her confessions rattled me in the best way possible. Then again, I didn't want to draw her mind away from her big interview.

Letting out a deep breath, I geared up to chat about anything, even the freaking weather, till Macy beat me to it.

"Listen, the other night, you mentioned having something to tell me." She paused, a moment so fleeting I barely noticed. "Wanna tell me now?"

Flustered, I found myself thrown by her baton pass—a green light to take the reins of our conversation, to guide us past awkwardness onto where we should have landed two nights ago.

"So," the information dump began with a subtle clearing of my throat, "me and—" I broke off, interrupted by the doorbell, my damn food delivery. "Hold that thought, okay?" Shooting up from the sofa, I shuffled to the door, phone still pinned to my ear. "Pretty sure pizza just arrived."

And when I swung the door open, my blood froze. "Oh...Harper."

10

Harper Kingston really knew how to rain—*hail* on a girl's parade.

"Hey, can I call you back?" Lucas snapped as if in a hurry.

I hated the whoosh of disappointment free-falling to my gut. Hated being *that* chick who got kicked to the curb, pushed to the side for another. Hated being jealous, envious of a perfect girl with a perfect face, perfect breasts, perfect just about everything, who probably pissed liquid gold and shit lambent diamonds.

Concealing the chagrin in my voice, I tossed him a brush-off, praying it exploded on impact. "Actually, let's catch up when I get back home. You've got a game coming up, and besides being tied up with all the interview business, I'll be hella busy doing 'single in New York City' stuff."

Hashtag boy bye.

Pressing the end-call button without giving him a second to reply, I felt hot, blood surging to my head, ticked-off at myself for not bossing the fuck up.

Over and done, I marched out of the bedroom and into the

living room of the posh, two thousand square-foot suite where my two besties were lounging on both couches.

Sage's nose was buried in her phone, while Chloe had hers in some museum tour brochure. Earlier, they'd wanted to go out for drinks and dancing, yet somehow play-it-safe-and-boring me convinced them it would be super fun if we ordered room service and hung out in our suite instead.

Seriously? What the hell was I thinking? We were in New Freaking York, the city that never sleeps. Deep down, I wanted to get out. Explore. Party my ass off. Meet someone who'd appreciate me. Be a book heroine and succumb to instalove, then smear my sexy hero all over Lucas Stone's annoyingly handsome face.

"Ladies," I said as I leaned against the granite-topped bar, arms folded across my chest, "we should totally head to that club you said everyone's raving about."

Chloe's gaze snapped to mine, neon-colored brochure in hand floating to the floor like a paper airplane. "Let's do it."

Sage's eyes widened, ears perked up like a chihuahua's, mouth fanned out in a grin as shit-eating as they come. "What changed your mind?"

"Well, I'm sick and tired of feeling like a goddamn poop emoji over someone who'll never be mine."

Both stared at me for a few beats, seemingly assessing my words, my mood, waiting to see if I would break down and cry or just go batshit and start throwing things.

"Wanna know something funny about that poop emoji?" Chloe tittered, sitting on the couch with her legs crossed yoga-style. "For the longest time, I thought that dark-brown swirly mound of cuteness was a chocolate frozen yogurt emoji. Stupid me texted a parade of poop emojis to a hottie who wanted to know my favorite dessert. I seriously wondered why he never texted me back."

We all laughed for a good sixty seconds before Sage got to her feet, skipping over to the bar, embracing me in a quick hug. "You deserve better, sweetie. Sure, there are times AJ can be an ass, but at least I know he's *my* ass. You need an ass who's all yours."

Nodding, I still had to nourish curiosity churning in my belly. "AJ hasn't mentioned anything to you about Lucas? Like, maybe that he'd read my confessions, or the fact we got close enough to kiss the other night?" I grabbed a bottle of water from the mini fridge, twisting the cap off before taking a sip.

"Girl, when I'm with AJ, there is absolutely no time to sit around and chat about other people's business—not when we're too busy fucking like a pair of manic bunnies."

I nearly spit my mouthful of water out. "It'll take a few drinks to rid my angelic mind free of visions of you and AJ going at it like a couple of horny rabbits."

"Same here," Chloe babbled, hands shielding her peepers as though AJ and Sage were in 3D hot-and-heavy right before her very eyes. "And don't forget to do a squat or two, Miss Shags Like a Bunny. Your dirty little mouth said *fucking* and *ass*."

About an hour later the three of us stood outside, wearing black, fashionably skimpy dresses and matching stilettos, ready and waiting in a line at Inkwell, a chic dance club and lounge other interviewees we ate lunch with earlier seemed wild about. Hip-hop music thumped, and everyone queued up behind the velvet ropes reminded me of those New York elites I'd read about in magazines.

I snapped a three-bestie selfie—our hair and makeup courtesy of Sage who watched a goin'-to-the-club beauty tutorial on YouTube—eager to upload it to UCChat when the line suddenly advanced. Tucking my cell into my sequined clutch, I beamed, euphoria gushing through me as we were ushered in.

Once inside, my eyes flicked to a starlit dance floor, rainbow-like rays bouncing from ceiling to floor. Stairs led upward to a lounge where two bars and plenty of tables, with cozy booths matching the club's velvet walls, were spread out. It would have been difficult to miss drop-dead-hot cocktail servers garbed in tuxedo-style corsets, sashaying about, trays of beers and sparkling drinks tactfully balanced on one hand as though they could carry out such skilled maneuvers while sleeping. Inkwell—packed with gorgeous men and women dancing, lounging, sipping drinks—definitely boomed, and as we stood at the entrance, taking everything in, I quickly surmised why other interns were nuts about it.

"Let's grab a booth." Sage snaked her way through a sea of party people, eventually leading me and Chloe up a mini flight of stairs to the lounge, the white dots that adorned her little black dress glowing under fluorescent lights.

Finding a wraparound booth off to the corner, the three of us eased in, clutches on our laps as we each picked up a drink menu from the marble-topped table.

"Stay away from Cosmos," Chloe teased, dishing me a cheeky side-eye. "No repeat episodes of real-life confessions."

"Hmm, the only real confession left to spill is how completely *over* Lucas Stone I truly am. And *Just Friends* would be its title because friend-boxed is what we're destined to be." I perused the menu, a plastic smile pulling at my lips.

Was I over Lucas?

Uh, that would be a big ass, no.

Though being way over him became this girl's mission, even if it meant cutting off circulation to my stupid heart.

Chasing away thoughts of Mr. Stone, I allowed myself to enjoy the moment with my bitches, music thrumming, vibrating through our booth. We probably looked similar to a set of bobble-heads as we sat there, grooving to sounds of kicked-up beats swirling around us.

"Hi, there. I'm Mindy." A chirpy-voiced cocktail server with dark lipstick stood in front of our booth, pen and pad in hand. "I'll be taking care of you dolls. Whatcha drinkin' tonight?"

Sage and Chloe took a final peek at their menus, then ordered Lemon Drops.

"And for you, hon?" Mindy eyed me, faux lashes fanning her face when she blinked. "Want the same?"

"Shirley Temple, please." I ignored the explosion of giggles erupting from Sage and Chloe's devious mouths.

"Sure thing, babe." Mindy scribbled on her pad. "Be right back with those."

Sage leaned back, arms crossed over her chest, lips pursed as if she'd just sucked a dozen limes. "Shirley Temple?"

"Mmhmm." I toyed with a loose strand of hair. "There's no way I'm walking into *Hot Shot* hung over tomorrow morning. I check in at seven-thirty."

Mindy dropped off our drinks, then showed us how to use the table-top kiosk to order more drinks, appetizers if we got hungry, and pay our bill when we're all done. "I'll come back to check on ya in a bit."

After playing with the kiosk, we ordered Inkwell's signature sliders and truffle fries basket. I fished my phone out of my purse to snap more selfies, then uploaded them to UCChat with #SingleInNewYork and #OutWithMyBitches.

"Holy Mother of Shit," Chloe squeaked, chin lifted in the direction of two guys walking toward us. "It's those hotties who sat across from our table at Pizza Express earlier today."

Slurping my sugary drink, I kept my gaze strapped to Chloe; snapping my eyes in their direction would have made it obvious we were talking about them. "So...they're stalking us?"

"We should be so lucky," Chloe snorted. "Those guys are here for interview week."

"And what makes you so sure about that, Ms. Nancy Drew?" Sage pestered.

"Because I saw them at our hotel. We were stepping off the elevator just as they stepped on. Both were holding that same *Welcome To Hot Shot* folder we got at check-in."

Truth is, I noticed them too—particularly the Chris Hemsworth clone who winked at me. But with no plans to hook up with some random hottie in New York, I ignored his silent greeting, and a few hours later, ignored a series of infectious smiles he flashed my way at Pizza Express.

Still, my heart burned.

I couldn't help but think meeting someone new could be the balm to soothe it.

"Sssh," Sage warned. "They're headed right for us."

Seconds later, I became enraptured by the sight and sound of absolute yumminess.

"Mind if we join you?"

11

LUCAS

"Here's your ring back," Harper gloated, mouth stretched out in an unabashed grin that told me she didn't give a single fuck. Apparently, the sleaze felt compelled to stop by and admit she'd been cheating on me for well over two years, dispatching her news with a nonchalant shrug.

Two. Years.

"Daddy likes you," she whined. "He wouldn't approve of me dating Sherlock, or anyone else from a rival team. I sort of used my relationship with you as a cover."

Tucking the ring in my sweatpants pocket, I didn't care for all the bullshit oozing from her mouth even though an inconsequential part of me wondered why she bothered saying yes to my marriage proposal.

Thankfully, while she stood in the doorway, yapping like Charlie Brown's teacher, that pizza delivery I'd been expecting showed up. I tipped the delivery guy, grabbed my food, then kicked the door closed, leaving Harper, jaw dropped and stupefied. When I sat down and dialed Macy, eager to finally disclose Harper and I were done, voicemail greeted me.

I'll be hella busy doing 'single in New York City' stuff.

Those words lingered, stuck to my brain like bubblegum to the bottom of a fucking shoe.

It didn't help matters when Sage posted pics of Macy seated *way* too close to some asshat with boy-band hair. KirkTheDream-Boat was the hashtag Sage used. Um...who the fuck was Kirk?

Three days later I found myself exhausted. Having had little to no sleep, my stomach, neck, whole body was in knots. Every single one of my calls to Macy went ignored, as did the numerous **call me back** text messages I'd sent. It became painfully—no, annoyingly—obvious she was giving me the brush-off.

AJ: Dude. Where the F are you? Practice started 20 minutes ago. Coach K is about to put out a bounty on your balls.

Fuck.

I'd played football most of my life and never had I been late to practice, especially one just two days before homecoming.

Me: On my way.

It took only ten seconds for his reply to swoosh in.

AJ: Whatever, fucker. Coach has us all doing sprints until you decide to show up.

Shitting bricks, I met nothing but red lights during my drive. By the time I walked onto the field, my teammates eyeballed me like a herd of angry sharks out for blood.

"Nice of you to join us, *Sir Lucas*." Coach K glanced at his watch, then fed me a death glare. "Your tardy-to-the-party ass has caused the team forty-five extra minutes of sprints."

Seemingly more brutal than normal, practice—the sprints, defensive tackles that knocked the wind out of me, offensive plays—grabbed me by the balls. My headspace, my thoughts, were in New York. Not hearing a peep from Macy fucked with me. I knew she was fine, alive, breathing, thanks to the never-ending slew of pictures posted on UCChat. But goddammit, she could've called, texted back.

After practice, a few of us went to Pancake Shack before our first class, and AJ's wisecrack candor only escalated my irritation toward Macy.

"You get a look at Macy's pics?" He shoved a forkful of scrambled eggs into his mouth. "Bro, it sure looks like she's met someone in New York."

As usual, he seemed oblivious to the fuck-off scowl I launched.

"Guy's not bad looking either," he babbled on as if enamored by the sound of his own voice. "I mean, for anyone into Thor look-alikes."

"Oh, you mean Kirk The Dreamboat?" Levi, the team's center quipped, fist over mouth. "That pic of him and Macy has been all over UCChat."

"Really?" I shrugged, cramming pancakes into my mouth. "Haven't noticed." *Liar.* "Been kinda busy mentally preparing for our game tomorrow," I added, the bold-faced lie larger than the long-standing rivalry between UCLA and Oregon State.

Truth is, my insides were ripped to shreds; visions of Macy meeting someone made me want to punch holes through walls.

"Guess you didn't tell Macy about you and Harper?" AJ poured ketchup over his hash browns, the smug told-ya-so grin on his face typical for someone who specialized in talking shit.

"Haven't had the chance considering she can't be reached." No longer interested in food that usually provided comfort, I tossed a handful of napkins over my plate.

"Wait. So, Mr. Lucas Almighty Stone's been ghosted?" Levi's shoulders quaked with laughter, and more teammates—Matt, Carter, Danny—joined his fist-over-mouth ha-ha bash.

Shaking my head, I shot up from the booth, ready to leave instead of smashing someone in two. "Whatever, shitbags. Y'all better be ready to beat the crap out of Sherlock Benson and his Ugly Ducklings Saturday."

12

MACY

"You've got quite the impressive academic résumé and the fact your mother is an investigative journalist and your dad a screenwriter, writing is definitely in your DNA." Chin tilted up, Kat Agassi, editor-in-chief of *Hot Shot* magazine blinked, her scarlet-stained lips pursed.

I swallowed, head bouncing up and down since, apparently, a simple phrase like "thank you" required a GPS guide to find its way out of my mouth.

Even though I knew I'd have a sappy fangirl moment during a face-to-face encounter with the periodical goddess, I didn't expect to sit there looking like some hybrid, deer-in-headlights-cat-got-your-tongue meme. Behind that ivory-colored desk, she resembled royalty perched on a throne. Chic. Intrepid. Badass. I swear, the queen bee of one of the world's most-read online magazine—second to *Cosmopolitan*—secreted the kind of confident swagger that would probably make someone like Beyoncé bow down and kiss the marble-tiled floor she floated on. An undeniable cross between Samantha Jones from *Sex and the City* and Miranda Priestly from *The Devil Wears Prada,* Kat rocked the hell out of her blond power bob, defined cheekbones, and flawless makeup.

Biting down on my lip, it became increasingly difficult to ignore the frantic drum of my heartbeat while feigning composure. *Breathe. Breathe. Breathe.*

Four days spent bouncing from department to department, surviving multiple panel interviews, it surprised me to learn I'd made an impression great enough to earn a place on Kat's list of candidates summoned for one-on-one time. Reaching this point in the interview process had felt like an eternity, and I wasn't ready to succumb to nervous defeat.

Kat's mocha-colored eyes crawled over me, narrowing into what seemed a lot like judgmental little slits. "Tell me, Ms. Sinclair, why is it I can't find any of your social media profiles?" She leaned back in her high-back chair, hands folded on her lap. "Here at *Hot Shot,* we scope out a candidate's Facebook, Insta, Snapchat, and Twitter accounts to make sure their posts, photos, hashtags don't in any way clash with our diverse and inclusive culture."

I swallowed, mouth dryer than the Sahara. "Actually, those profiles were deleted about four years ago under the advice of my academic advisor."

Kat's pencil-thin brows traveled north the same time her mouth curved into a kittenish smirk. "Oh? And why is that?"

"Well, UCLA devised its own social media platform, UCChat. It's a blend of Facebook, Instagram, Snapchat, and Twitter. The university highly encourages students to use that instead of any of the other four." I sat up tall, legs crossed, an unexpected boost of self-confidence morphing me into Chatty Cathy. "This way, should we share or post something foolish during our crazy college years —I'm sure you can relate—they don't come back to haunt us later, like when we're busy trying to score a good-paying job, putting our hard-earned degrees to use."

Kat said nothing at first, her inexpressive gaze steamrolling my confidence. "Smart of you to heed their advice. We turn away more than qualified applicants every day after coming across something they'd deemed trivial at the time of posting. Even trivial things could end up being detrimental to *Hot Shot's* brand if discovered."

I smiled timidly, feeling there must've been something she was leading up to. Did she come across something from my past?

Avoiding her unreadable assessment, my eyes roamed the larger-than-life office, cruising past its floor-to-ceiling Park Avenue view, walls adorned with blown-up cover photos of *Hot Shot's* issues, before landing back on Kat's evaluating perusal.

My phone bleeped, an all-too-familiar tone I meant to mute that morning.

Lucas. Stone.

He'd been calling and texting me nonstop, obviously failing to read the big-ass *I'm-ignoring-the-heck-out-of-you* memo that should have been clear as day. I figured he'd probably caught sight of pictures Sage posted of me and Kirk—the hottie Chris Hemsworth clone. Turned out, the *other* hottie with him was actually his partner. Those photos? Staged. All orchestrated to make Lucas *assume* I'd met someone. He needed to focus on his fiancée, while I needed time to let my heart breathe, slowly ease out of love with someone it had no business falling for in the first place.

"Sorry," I tittered, rummaging through my purse, determined to strangle the phone that just kept on beeping. "It's my roommate—"

"Lucas Stone? The drool-worthy morsel of hunky-hotness who's been your best friend since forever?"

I blinked up, jaw practically in my lap. "Um...yeah?"

Kat chuckled, head leaning like the Tower of Pisa. "See, while searching for you on social media channels, I came across your book blog." She lifted a piece of paper from off her desk. "*Confessions of a Bookaholic?*"

My breath hitched, and not in the way it happens for so many book heroines.

"Your blog is genius, relevant for this age when romance novels breathe life into women—*and men*—who crave an escape from their everyday world. Three weeks ago I subscribed to your blog, even downloaded the app, as a part of our vetting process before granting the HR team approval to extend a welcome to interview for our winter internship."

Putting two and two together, my cheeks felt hot, embarrassment plunging to the pit of my already nerve-rattled stomach. "So, you must have read..."

"Your digital diary," she finished, gaze switching from unreadable to warm. "I loved how readers, *fans*, thousands of followers, gave you a virtual hug, flooding your blog with such uplifting, supportive comments and, oh, my gosh"—she held her belly while containing her laugh—"those who thought it was an exclusive excerpt from an upcoming novel simply made my day."

Failing to grasp what was going on I said, "I do have some of the best followers."

"Indeed, you do. Readers flock to bloggers they feel a connection with. Someone real, authentic, relatable, whose novel choices aren't influenced by one, or all, of the big-five publishing houses who they may indirectly sponsor. I've gone back and read your reviews, and appreciate how you've critiqued, not only books by traditionally published authors like Nora Roberts, Danielle Steel, and Nicholas Sparks, but also by indie authors whose literary talent sometimes goes unnoticed."

Kat rose from her chair, red-bottomed heels click-clacking against the pricey floor as she made her way over to the window. Letting out a sigh, she crossed her arms while peering out at New York City. "I've teetered back and forth with ideas of adding a book review column to *Hot Shot* for quite some time now, trying to decide what would be the appropriate platform, the perfect tie-in to our chic and well-represented brand." She spun around, face beaming brighter than a thousand suns. "Which is why I'm prepared to offer you and your fabulous creation, *Confessions of a Bookaholic,* a full-time position at *Hot Shot.*"

"*WHAT*?" Sage bit into an egg roll, wide green eyes nearly jumping out of her head. "She offered you a *job*, job?"

"Well," I cautioned, swallowing a forkful of chicken fried rice. The three of us were eating dinner at *Sun Sai Gai,* the last stop on our New York City touristy-things-to-do list. "Of course, nothing comes easy. I'll need to charm investors and board members by pitching a plan that construes how *Confessions of a Bookaholic* will bring more readers to *Hot Shot.*"

Chloe slurped egg drop soup into her mouth, shoulders shimmying in excitement. Working for a well-known magazine had been our dream and I was one step closer to living it out. "Oh, my gosh! See? Sage and I knew only good things would come out of your one-on-one with *the* Kat Agassi." She paused, curiosity knitting her brows together. "Wait, when is this presentation thingy supposed to happen? I mean, we fly back home early tomorrow morning."

I explained how a few candidates—myself included—were to remain in New York for the weekend, all working collectively on a presentation for our group pitch to investors and board members Monday morning.

"So, you're gonna skip tomorrow night's homecoming game?" Sage asked, mouth pouting.

The reality of missing the game—especially one against a long-standing rival—painted a ring of guilt around my heart. "Yes, but I'm sure I can stream it on UCChat."

"Well, girl, you deserve the *fuck* out of this," Sage said, chopsticks pointed in my direction. "And, please"—she glared at Chloe—"don't you dare tell me to do squats. After this long-ass week, unleashing that F-bomb felt better than sex."

13

LUCAS

"Tonight's just another game." Coach K stood in the middle of our pregame huddle, his scruffy voice, brawny power pose in full effect. "But, let's remind these assholes whose house they're in."

Homecoming.

Normally, it would've been no big deal to me.

But this one?

This homecoming represented the end of an era, my last big college game—apart from playoffs—before getting drafted by the National Football League.

Roars filled Rose Bowl Stadium, our marching band inciting fans with UCLA's Fight song, and as we were finally announced, chills coursed through my veins, a sea of blue and gold cheers erupting in the stands as fans welcomed us onto the field.

Bruins! Bruins! Bruins! Bruins!

God, I loved our fans. They had this undeniable spirit that could fuel an army, carry a brigade of gladiators to battle, and homecoming games had a tendency to draw in a combination of fans, old and new. Everyone I knew was mounted in those stands: my parents, classmates, frat bros, professors, friends, frenemies.

Everyone.

Except Macy.

Hey, not going to make tonight's game. Got tied up in New York. I'll watch via UCChat since they won't be playing it here on TV. Good luck!

Macy's text pinched my heart.

Four days of radio silence and *that's* the text she decided to grace me with twenty minutes before kickoff? As far as I knew, she was supposed to board a plane early that morning with ample time in between for traditional pregame tailgating and shenanigans—which I'd assumed she'd been doing with Sage and Chloe as usual.

Tied up in New York.

Right.

For what?

With who?

Kirk? Fuck him.

Rage engulfed me—not toward her. Toward myself.

You should have at least told her you ended shit with Harper before she left.

Had I done what AJ said, Macy probably wouldn't be on the eastern seaboard falling for *Captain Kirk.*

Regardless, I never bothered texting her back. Didn't want her to know how much it mattered that she wasn't there. How much I craved her presence. How much she'd been missed over the last four days, nights packed with dreams of her riding my cock.

"Heads." Sherlock Benson stood across from me at coin toss, a smugger-than-fuck scowl etched into his ugly face.

The referee flipped a coin, shiny silver spinning in what felt like slow motion, until it bounced to its death on the green.

"Tails," announced zebra-man, making fans go wild with roaring excitement.

I strapped my helmet on, shouldering past Sherlock who pestered, "Bet you were shocked I was *really* fucking your girl."

"Oh, you mean the slut who probably kissed you after having my cock in her mouth?"

Sherlock hoofed toward me, the referee stepping between us, palms pressed against our jerseys. "Really, guys? Save this soap-opera-grade skirmish for off the field before you both receive a penalty."

Fists clenched, I jogged over to my team, inner voice reminding myself beating the crap out of that bag of dicks wasn't worth a personal foul resulting in an ejection from the game.

"You okay?" AJ whacked the top of my helmet, eyes reading my expression. Our years-long friendship had gifted him the ability to recognize when my blood reached its boiling point, and God knows he'd been one to stop me from losing my shit when a rival's trash talk cut close to home.

"Yep." I pounded my fists together. "We need to win."

"C'mon, bro. You know damn well we've got this."

First quarter ended up being a cinch, a touchdown keeping us in the lead, and at the end of our first half, we were in our zone, owning the gridiron, ahead by double digits.

"All right, guys. Listen up." Inside the locker room, Coach K commanded the team's attention, scaling us down from our victorious high. "We've still got two quarters left and you know damn well those quackers are in there, reviewing our last scoring plays." He leaned against a row of lockers, brows knitted, arms folded over his chest. "Don't. Get. Comfortable. This game is ours to win or ours to lose, depending on where your heads are. Stay focused and don't dick around. And linemen"—he eyeballed Danny, Matt, Carter, Jordan, and Todd—"keep watch; their pass rushes have been getting a little too close to Lucas."

Energized and focused, we pretty much dominated the second half, triumphant pride puffing our chests out. Thanks to a sweet, eighteen-point lead, we'd more than earned rights to claim dibs on trash talk, and during a fourth-quarter pre-snap formation, Levi spit out, "You on your period today?" to the Ducks' three-hundred-fifty-pound defensive tackle before snapping me the ball.

Surprisingly, the Ducks stayed quiet, not a single one of them visibly roused by Levi's heckling.

After catching his snap, I spotted AJ, ran back a couple feet, ready to pass him the pigskin when I got slammed into from behind, air escaping my lungs, shockwaves of pain tapping nerves in my body as I hit the ground.

And everything went black.

14

MACY

et up, Lucas.

Please... Get. The. Hell. Up.

Pain gripped the walls of my chest as I watched UCChat's live stream, Lucas on the field facedown and motionless after getting tackled by a monster-truck-sized Duck—their defensive end crashing into him from behind.

Players and coaches from both sides surrounded Lucas as UCLA's medical support staff shoved their way through, promptly trying to access their fallen quarterback hero.

I shot out of bed, pacing, eyes pinned to my iPad in hand, mind and conscience besieged with a squadron of guilt-ridden should-haves.

Should have been there.

Should have been in the stands.

Should have been in Los Angeles chasing, *fighting for* Lucas instead of in New York chasing some stupid dream like a kid chases her shadow.

Why isn't he moving?

Acting on autopilot, I set my iPad onto the bed, then plucked my cell phone off the nightstand beside it. Hands shaking, I fired off a group text to Sage and Chloe.

Me: What's happening!?

Sage: Um...

Chloe: Can't see. Everyone is surrounding him. But, it doesn't look good. We heard the collision from where we're sitting in the stands.

Chloe followed her text with a handful of crying-face emojis just as my heart collapsed.

Me: I'm coming home.

∽

THE WORLD, and everything in it, moves at a snail's pace when you're trying to get somewhere.

Ubers.

Lines at the airport.

Airplanes.

Five hours into my flight back to Los Angeles and I swear the pilot must have taken us on a scenic route up to the moon, around the sun, past Timbuktu, and everywhere in between.

Leg bouncing, I eagerly awaited news from Sage and Chloe. Thanks to airplane Wi-Fi, their sporadic information drops kept me mildly sane, although their last major update—sent several hours ago—triggered a surge of anxiety.

Lucas had suffered a grade three, maybe even a grade four, concussion.

Turning to Google for insight on different concussion grades and what they meant only intensified the already tsunami-like waves of panic coursing through me. And from what I'd discovered on reputable medical sites, concussions of any magnitude could lead to brain damage.

"More ginger ale?"

The flight attendant's chirpy voice came out of nowhere, causing me to squeal.

"Sorry, I didn't mean to frighten you, hon," she assured, sympathy framing her face. "We're just doing our last rounds of service."

Flustered, I set my phone onto the tray table, nodding in acceptance of her offer. "How long before we land?"

"About forty-five minutes." Her eyes combed over my face. "You should rest, seeing how you've been awake since we left New York. Everyone usually sleeps during a red-eye." She opened a can of soda, its hiss echoing through the mostly empty flight. "Here you go," she said as she set it down beside my phone on the tray table. "I'll be back in a bit to collect your trash."

Bubbles tickled my throat as I sipped the cold drink, downing it as though I were some parched wanderer, stranded in the desert without a droplet of water.

Setting the cup onto the tray, I lifted the window shade, my gaze adjusting to bright rays of sunlight cascading above a sea of puffy clouds. Nearly 5 a.m.—I'd spent the majority of the flight texting, reading, *worrying* when I should have been sleeping like the flight attendant said. My whole body ached with concern. I needed to see Lucas, needed to know that he was okay. Needed to find the courage to tell him it was impossible to fall out of love with him.

"LET me help you with your bag." An Uber driver wearing dark shades and a USC T-shirt hopped out of the car, circling around it to pull my luggage from the opened trunk.

Arriving at UCLA Medical Center just after 7 a.m., I had no clue where to go. Sage and Chloe were unreachable, likely fast asleep, and my parents, who were close friends with Lucas's, barely knew which floor he was on.

Suitcase in tow, I shuffled through the glass sliding doors, nervous tension whirling in my belly like a hurricane. Menacing thoughts, god-forbidding scenarios—*was he badly injured, sedated, unconscious*—had me in knots; tears I'd been able to hold back were dying to burst free as I charged, chin up, toward the elevators.

He's on floor two.

It's what my mom told me, and during the elevator ride up it became difficult to breathe, heart-wrenching dread slithering through me.

At the nurses' station, I asked where his room was, fingertips tapping the counter, eyes scanning the wing as if I'd figure it out on my own.

"Lucas Stone," a gray-haired nurse coughed out, keying his name into the computer, eyeglasses perched on the tip of her nose. "Only one visitor at a time, and I believe another young woman is already in there with him."

Harper Kingston. Why wouldn't she be with her man? I mean, they were soon to be married. Of course, she was by his side, sitting right where I would have handed over half my soul to be.

"I'll just wait in the visitor's lounge then?" My rattled nerves had me spit it out like an action that required her approval.

"Sure. Just check back here in about twenty minutes."

Only me and a television mounted high up against the wall sat in the lounge, and since I didn't care to watch *Health News Today*, I fished my cell and headphones from my bag, plugging one of the buds into my right ear, skimming through the many playlists on Spotify. Drake played, escorting me to times Lucas rapped along whenever he showered, the memories curling a smile on my face. Leaning back, I closed my eyes, beats casting a sense of calm into a whirlwind of worry.

"Macy?"

Eyes sprung open, my head snapped to the oh-so-familiar voice.

Lucas's mother.

"Oh, sweetheart. So glad you made it." She walked over toward me, arms fanned out, and I got right to my feet, meeting her halfway, the two of us locking in an embrace. "How long have you been here?"

I pulled back, offering a one-shoulder shrug. "Maybe ten, fifteen minutes? How's Lucas?"

She took hold of my hand, guiding me toward the door. "I'll be more than happy to give you all the details later. But, why not head on over to Lucas first? He's in room 202. Take your time. I can stay here with your suitcase and read a book until you get back."

Hesitation halted my tracks. "One of the nurses told me he had a visitor. I really don't wanna walk in on him and Harper."

"No, honey. *I* was the one with Lucas." Confusion seemed to crease her forehead. "Why would you think *Harper*, of all people, would be visiting him?"

I blinked.

"Wait," she interrupted. "You don't know?"

"Know...what?" My bottom lip quivered.

She stepped close, warm palm cupping my cheek. "Lucas broke up with that horrible Harper Kingston last week—the same day your sweet, tell-all diary went viral." She smiled sincerely, eyes the same steel blue as her son's boring into mine. "Honey, go see him. He's been asking for you."

Pulling the door open, I ran, unsure if my feet were pounding the floor in the right direction, missing a collision with a cart pushed by a custodian who fussed at me to slow down.

I passed room 196, 198, 200 and as my hand twisted the doorknob to open room 202, I exhaled.

"Hey." An unforgettable, breath-stealing blend of surprise and elation lined Lucas Stone's ridiculously handsome features.

"Hey," I replied, taking slow, tentative strides closer to him even though I really wanted to run over and smother him with twelve thousand kisses.

God, he looked perfectly delish, outfitted in standard hospital threads and a coquettish smirk that made my heart pitter-patter loud enough, he must've heard it once I made it over to the side of his hospital bed.

Grabbing hold of my hand, Lucas drew me near, piercing gaze swaying with mine. "So"—his voice sounded gruff, surprisingly sexy for someone newly concussed—"what the heck took you so long?"

15

LUCAS

My father used to say bumps in the road were springboards skyrocketing us closer to our dreams. As a kid, that parental proverb lacked substance, meaning; however, as I crept further into adulthood, Dad's inspirational phrase meant everything.

After the doctor told me there'd be no football for at least two or three weeks, I was shattered. Two weeks sans football meant I'd miss playoff games, miss closing out our winning season, and most importantly, miss scouts in the stands scoping me out as a potential prospect.

Coach K and Dad reminded me scouts attend the NFL Combine—a predraft event I'd received an invitation to over summer break. That in mind, I decided to view my concussion as a positive. That bump in the road needed to springboard me closer to my dream. Macy.

With weeks absent from the gridiron, I'd have no early morning practices, no traveling out-of-state for games against Oregon, Oklahoma, or Texas, no rigorous workouts that made me too burned out to breathe. Instead, I'd have time alone with Macy —time to learn if we had what it takes to mold our forever-long friendship into something palpable, something real, something *romantic*.

I'd already fallen head over everything for Macy, my best friend—a kind of adoration that was unconditional, safe, treasured.

But, holy fuck.

Falling for Macy as my girlfriend, my lover? I couldn't wait.

Well, after I made sure Kirk the Jerk was out of the picture.

Dotted with tears, Macy's long lashes fluttered, full lips curving into a sassy, hitched-up mouth that never failed to make my cock twitch.

"What took me so long?" she huffed. "Did you expect me to teleport myself here? The flight took six hours, silly, and believe me," she said as she blinked up, wiping away one lone tear trickling down her cheek, "I got here as fast as I could."

"Hey, look at me." I squeezed her wrist, waiting until her blue eyes flicked back to mine. "No tears, okay? I'm fine, promise. Doc said grade three is common and I just need to rest up. Take it easy over the next couple of weeks."

She surveyed the monitors, the IV in my arm. "What exactly does 'take it easy' mean?"

"No football, strenuous activity, exercise, or school for two, possibly three weeks."

Her brows took a hike upward. "In other words, you'll be at home, annoying the heck out of me twenty-four-seven?"

"Exactly. And you know I've a tendency to put one-hundred percent into everything I do, right?" I winked, loving how cute she looked, head tilted, cheeks suddenly beaming a bright shade of pink.

When she sat down beside me, the body-to-body contact, even through hospital bedding, ignited sparks between us. "Your mom told me about you and Harper."

"I wanted to break the news, but you went to New York, then met Jerk—"

"Kirk," she corrected, her giggles like an angelic melody. "He has a *boyfriend*"—she paused, gaze reading my relieved reaction —"and besides that, he's not my type."

Licking my lips, I wondered if kissing her mouth would be off-limits during my recovery. "And...who's your type?"

"Lucas Stone?"

We both jumped, the untimely intrusion catching us caught off guard. "It's time for your MRI."

Pretty sure there's nothing worse than having a moment destined for at least one smooch sidelined by someone ready to cart you off for a head X-ray.

"Can you stay a little while longer?" I dished a set of puppy-dog eyes. "My MRI shouldn't take too long. I'd love to hear all about New York."

Thirty minutes later, Macy sat crossed-legged in a chair beside my hospital bed, bright-eyed and animated, delivering a play-by-play of her trip to the Big Apple. It didn't go unnoticed how she spoke mostly of things she got into with Sage and Chloe, skirting around details about why she went there in the first place.

"And what about the interview? Was it everything you imagined?"

She nodded vigorously, tugging a loose strand of hair behind her ear. "Mmm-hmm. It was great."

"Okay...when will you know if you've been accepted to their winter internship?"

Her eyes sprang to the ceiling. "A few weeks, I suppose?"

Silence swallowed the room, save for the monitor keeping track of my heart rate, beats faster than they were before Macy walked in.

"Why'd you get tied up? Did you miss Saturday's early morning flight?"

Macy explained she'd been part of a group asked to complete one more assignment. After I asked if she'd been able to get it done, all she said was "Yep," changing the subject when she added, "When will you be discharged?"

"They want to keep me at least twenty-four hours for observation. Since I got here after nine last night, I suppose I'll go home sometime tonight."

Getting to her feet, she smiled. "I should probably go get your mom. She's been waiting with my luggage. Plus I'd like to go home and shower."

"Doc wants to be sure someone at home can monitor me for at least another twenty-four hours, then kind of watch over me for the next two weeks. Will you be able to do that? Or should I stay with my parents instead?"

She padded over, resting her hand on my chest, leaning in as her soft lips brushed against my forehead. "Of course, I'll be able to."

Sauntering her way out, Macy left me staring at her ass, panting like a ravenous wolf.

$\sim$

"No strenuous exercise means no sex or anything else that will increase your heart rate, understood?" Doctor Mead's stern expression made me nervous. "I mean it, Lucas. Even if you feel fine, don't push it. We'll evaluate you again after one week."

Waiting to be discharged, I sat on the hospital bed's edge, staring down at my sneakers, hating the asshole defensive end who slammed into me. "Okay, I get it. Nothing but rest, rest, and more rest."

"It's only temporary, Son." Dad squeezed my shoulder. "Next thing you know, everything will be back to normal."

"He's right," Mom chimed in. "And if you'd rather come back home for recovery, I'll take time off work and—"

"Mom, it's fine," I stopped her mid-sentence. "You don't need to take time off, and Dad doesn't need to cancel his trip to Vegas. Macy will be with me, and since she's got online studies, I don't expect she'll even need to leave the house."

"And Macy is..." Doctor Mead wrinkled his nose.

"My best friend." *Who I happen to be crazy about.*

"Is she the blonde who was in here with you earlier? Because the nurses all joked about how your heart rate sped up the whole time she was in here, then settled back down a few minutes after she left." He chuckled, noting something on my chart. "Just be sure to keep things *friendly* between the two of you while you recover."

"Not even one kiss?" I asked on behalf of my impatient lips, curious to know how Macy tasted.

"If all best friends looked like her, one kiss wouldn't be enough."

16

"You didn't tell him about the job offer?" Sage's wide eyes zapped me with unapproving judgment during our three-way FaceTime chat.

"Why would I? Seeing how Yours Truly packed up and left, that offer no longer exists." I peeled an onion and set it onto the kitchen counter beside the rest of the ingredients: garlic, carrots, and celery I'd set out to dice. Lucas loved my chicken noodle soup, and I figured it would be a nice, comforting meal to surprise him with once he got home.

"It's Sunday afternoon," Chloe said. "You can still fly back to New York and make it in time for tomorrow's presentation."

She wasn't wrong.

It would have been easy for me to hop on a plane and make that interview, especially since the group I was with finished our presentation preparations Saturday. However, I couldn't leave Lucas, not when he needed me. Sure, the opportunity Kat Aggasi offered was my wish come true. Even so, Lucas was my *dream* come true and according to Walt Disney, a dream is a wish your heart makes.

I ran the knife through the onion, chopping like a Martha

Stewart pro. "Can't fly back to New York, considering I promised Lucas I'd monitor him for the next twenty-four hours and be here for him throughout the rest of his recovery."

"Um...helloooo?" Sage brought her index finger to the screen, tapping it three times. "Anyone home? Can't Harper do that? She's his effing fiancée."

"Lucas broke up with her the day my stupid diary got smeared everywhere."

I set the knife down to capture a screenshot of Sage and Chloe's jaw-dropped expressions.

"Well, fuck me to the moon." Chloe sighed, eyes gleaming.

"Yeah...what she said," Sage babbled, hand over heart. "Then, you're right. You need to stay. I'm sure another magazine opportunity will come around soon."

The prospect curved my lips upward, hopeful what she said held a grain of truth.

After ending our call, I continued my meal prep, dicing, and mincing veggies to use for the soup. Lucas wasn't expected home for another few hours, which allowed plenty of time for me to cook then shower. I'd been too tired to shower when I got home hours earlier, opting to catch up on sleep lost during the flight.

Before I knew it, Lucas and his parents—Todd and Staci—sat around the oak kitchen table with me, all four of us feasting on chicken noodle soup. I'd invited his mom and dad to stay for dinner, considering it was close to 8 p.m. when they brought him home from the hospital. Besides that, my nerves had me on edge. The realization of being *alone* with Lucas—*the newly single Lucas, thank you very much*—had my mind whirling, unanswered questions about our future at the forefront.

Fact is, I'd read shit tons of friends-to-lovers romance novels, each time imagining Lucas was the hot hero and I the sassy heroine, my heart swooning over a real-life possibility. Yet, everyone knows romance reads are fluffy ever-after tales with guaranteed happy endings that don't happen in true life.

Hope slid to the bottom of my gut, reality making me question whether or not Lucas and I could become something more without jeopardizing the bulletproof relationship we'd constructed over the years. If we dove in, trusting our desires alone, would things be different or could we manage to keep our relationship the same, adding a splash of romance as a benefit? Or, when we finally kissed—and, let's face it, that moment seemed inevitable—what if the chemistry I dreamed about wasn't there?

To be honest, Lucas was a badass best friend. Loyal. Trustworthy. *Protective*.

My idea of Lucas as a boyfriend was just as badass. Hot. Irresistible. *Yummy*.

But, suppose we didn't work out as a couple? Fear of possibly losing my best friend erected a mile-wide wall of doubt around my heart.

"Thanks for dinner, sweetie." Staci stood near the front door, shouldering into her sweater. "You'll have to tell me your recipe."

I chuckled. "You can get it from my mom. It's her not-so-secret recipe."

"I'll remember that when we chat tomorrow about our annual cruise. Can you believe it's that time of year already?" She kissed me on the cheek, then looked over to her husband, who was sitting on the couch going over recovery tips with Lucas. "Honey? Are you ready to go?"

Hugs were exchanged, and I offered reassurance that I'd keep a watchful eye on their son.

"Believe me, we have no doubt Lucas is in good hands," Todd said, rocking back on his feet.

"And don't forget, I've arranged for some groceries to be delivered tomorrow," Staci added, before they both gave a final wave goodbye.

Lucas showered while I cleaned the kitchen and once that task was completed, I—or *Nurse Macy* as Lucas teased earlier—padded over to his bedroom to make sure the injured patient had everything he needed for the night.

Bottled water in hand, I knocked one time before Lucas swung the bedroom door open, nothing but a towel around his waist.

To say I stood there gawking at everything on display—his massive chest, abs of steel, a happy trail that steered my gaze southbound to an impressive bulge—would be an understatement. My eyes devoured—correction, they *gobbled*—every bit of Lucas Stone, like a team of ravenous Pac-Mans munching away on those teeny-tiny dots.

"I was about to get ready for bed," he said, droplets of water dancing on his skin.

"Wa-wa," I babbled, my idiot mouth getting a little too acquainted with my foot.

"Wa-wa?" He arched a brow.

Swallowing, I brandished the bottle of water in hand, foggy brain recalling that offering it to him was the reason I stood in the doorway distracted by one helluva glorious-looking body. "*Water*...would you like some water?"

His smirk disclosed how much my sudden case of foolishness amused him. "Everything okay? Or should I be the one watching over you tonight instead?"

Fighting back a smile, I rolled my eyes. "Obviously, your concussion hasn't affected your propensity to be a smart-ass."

"Looks like the blow may have only intensified it."

Brash. Sexy. Concussed. Jerk.

"Here." I shoved the bottled water into his rock-hard chest. "When I come back in five minutes, please be fully dressed. Apparently, I can't concentrate when your naked chest and abs, *among other things*, are slapping me senseless."

I marched to my bedroom, changed out of jeans and a sweat-shirt into shorts and a T-shirt, then shuffled into the bathroom across the hall to brush my teeth. Five minutes later, I was greeted by a fully dressed Lucas, also wearing shorts and a T-shirt, his face still garnished with that irresistible cocky charm.

"You should probably get some rest," I suggested, leaning up against his bedroom door frame.

"I'd thought we'd go over some of the aftercare instructions the hospital provided."

I nodded, treading into his bedroom, settling onto the foot of his bed. "What's it say?"

He eased down beside me, and my heart fluttered when a soft dusting of hairs on his thighs tickled mine. "Well, no strenuous exercise, of course, and I'll need plenty of rest. It also says I can sleep uninterrupted now, but when I'm awake, you'll have to be on the lookout for any of these symptoms." He handed me the hospital's discharge instructions.

The list of symptoms, which included drowsiness or difficulty waking up, trouble walking, talking, concentrating, and constant headaches, solidified how serious an injury he sustained. In his eyes, I sensed vulnerability, despite his strong facade. "Lucas, are you scared?"

He shook his head. "No. I mean, well, at first I was, yes. Waking up on the field, not being able to remember what happened, only to be carted off the field and into an ambulance?" He stroked his jaw. "Shit, Macy, I didn't know what the fuck was going on. I only knew that my head hurt like hell and there was a ringing in my ears making me want to barf for days."

Resting the palm of my hand on his thigh, I said, "I'm so sorry I wasn't there."

"Hey." He tipped my chin up with the gentle graze of his thumb, heart-melting gaze and voice soft and consoling. "You aren't the asshat who slammed into me. Besides, you're here now."

His words were breathless, and so desperately I wanted to lean in, brush his lips with mine. But my desire quickly died, laid to rest by a pesky case of doubt buzzing around my heart like a mosquito at a backyard BBQ. "Other than looking out for these symptoms, what else can I do to help?"

It seemed as though a million ideas stormed through his gorgeous eyes. "Sleep with me tonight."

17

LUCAS

"You want me to sleep with you?" Macy's cheeks turned the color of Mars.

"Get your head out of the gutter, *Nurse Macy.*"

She straightened, chin defensively tilted up. "Maybe you're the one whose head is in the gutter."

True.

I wanted nothing more than to have Macy Sinclair stripped down and beautiful between the sheets, my hands, mouth, and cock exploring every millimeter of her. The doctor's orders of no strenuous activity included sex, which meant a naked Macy in my bed was out of bounds for at least two weeks.

Fuck.

"Look, I figured you can curl up beside me like you usually do after we watch an episode of Dexter."

"You mean like I *used* to do? Because we haven't watched Dexter for over three years," she quipped, arms folded over her chest.

"Anyone ever tell you how adorable you look when you're being sassy?"

"Anyone ever tell you not to use the word *adorable* when describing a grown-ass woman?"

I chuckled, all too aware when it came to us, there never seemed to be a dull moment, our banter like nothing I'd experienced with anyone else. "All kidding aside, will you please stay with me tonight? Sleep beside me? It'll make me feel more comfortable to know you're here just in case I'm not feeling well in the middle of the night."

Blue eyes searched mine, and for a second I thought her sexy mouth would ooze more of that highly-addictive sass. "Yes, I'll stay with you tonight."

Thank. You. God.

As the hours ticked by, Macy and I lay in bed chatting, laughing, and reminiscing about stuff we got into when we were young and even things we did in our teens. The room was dark and outside was quiet, save for the sky's night light seeping in from the window blinds and crickets chirping in the distance.

Even though my bed was king-sized, Macy curled up beside me, close enough for me to hear—*feel* her murmured breaths, smell her flowery shampoo, catch moments when her lashes fluttered, the temptation to touch her almost unbearable. She was a bombshell package. Gorgeous. Alluring. Smart. I mentally kicked the fool I'd been over the years for not making a move on her, regardless of some dimwitted pact we'd endorsed as a pair of naive little kids.

"Remember, prom?" I asked, practically hearing her eyes roll in disgust.

"Oh my gosh, yes. How could I forget? You went all batty when my date and I headed up the elevator to his hotel room."

"Batty? I was only trying to protect you."

"From what? Becoming a prom-night cliché? First of all," she huffed, "I never planned on doing anything with him. Second of all, I wasn't about to lose my virginity to Derek Thompson when I was saving it for—" She stopped talking, releasing a breath as she abruptly shifted from her side, onto her back.

"You were saving it for...?"

She shifted, the two of us face to face again. "Why did you break up with Harper?"

Changing the subject had always been her specialty, and I answered the question as though her script flip didn't bug me. "Well, I went to Harper's house to end things, then caught her stripping for Sherlock Benson."

"Wait. *Stripping* for Sherlock Benson?" She giggled. "Holy. Fuck."

"Tell me about it," I said, thinking the irony of it all was actually funny.

"But, you said you'd gone there to end things anyway. Why?"

The one-worded question forced me up against two options: either become a shifty subject-changer like her or start a conversation about that blog post, paving a clear path back to the discussion we should have had before she left for her week-long interview in New York.

Which option did I choose? The one that took care of the elephant in the room.

"To be honest, I decided to break up with Harper after reading your blog post."

The sound of her, my, *our* rapid heartbeats galloped around us, and it seemed as though the world stopped turning, seconds in time completely frozen while Macy digested my words.

"And you decided that because...?" Her voice trailed off to a sexy, purr-like whisper that made my cock twitch.

I inched near, closing the small space between us, my lips fanning hers. "Because, Macy Sinclair"—my fingers gripped her waist, the subtle, barely-there touch making her whimper—"I'm in love with you, have been since forever. Your blog post, your confession helped me realize I'd been too damn stupid to admit it." Mouth parted, I had to kiss her, taste her, feel her. Slowly. Gently. A kiss worthy of mending all the years I'd wasted not kissing her, not tasting her sweet tongue as it danced with mine.

Lips easing onto hers, the first brush started out tentative, explorative, quickly becoming hungry and hot, me—*maybe both of us*—craving more. She drifted onto her back, an open invitation for me to settle on top, our mouths never separating, too eager, too desperate to make up for years wondering how *everything* this moment would be. God, how good it felt to have her under me, fingers feverishly diving through my hair, legs hugging my waist, hips slowly, methodically rocking.

"*Shit, Macy,*" I groaned, cock hard, so ready to score its own delectable meet and greet.

If not for doctor's orders, our first kiss could have easily become our first fuck. I'd always wondered, always knew it would be good, but I didn't expect our kiss to be better than I imagined. It left me smitten, *ruined* to the point of no return.

"No strenuous exercise," she panted out, and I couldn't help but smirk.

"Then why are you tugging at the bottom of my T-shirt?"

Her lips curved up against mine, a light giggle trickling free. "Obviously, my hands have a mind of their own."

I dropped a line of soft kisses along the delicate slope of her neck, ignited by the hum of her moans vibrating against my tongue and mouth.

Working my way to the shell of her ear, I whispered, "I've imagined tasting your sweet lips plenty of times." I kissed a path back to her mouth, locking lips once more with the woman who made my heart shake. "When the doctor clears me, I plan on taking my time tasting the sweet lips between your thighs, like I've also imagined doing plenty of times."

It would be two weeks before the doctor cleared me, and I

couldn't help but wonder how the fuck I'd be able to wait that long.

18

MACY

My heart hiccuped, tipsy after just one kiss from Lucas Stone.

So many parts of me were on fire, starving for more. His full lips on mine, the feel of his cock pressed up against my center, the moment I'd dreamed of probably eleventy-thousand times, mesmerized the hell out of me.

I hadn't expected to hear Lucas tell me he was in love with me, nor did I expect our first kiss would happen while lying in his bed, each instance leaving me feeling like my heart had taken a speedboat to the moon.

It wasn't easy to stop, derailing our collective desire that had us panting, bodies molded, eager to take more explorative leaps and bounds, yet we knew we had to, both unwilling to risk Lucas further injury.

When the doctor clears me, I plan on taking my time tasting the sweet lips between your thighs...

Swoon. Magic. And it took the whole rest of the night to calm down after he hummed those words, my sex begging me to at least allow Mr. Stone, my trusty vibrator, the opportunity to pacify my needs.

Watching him drift off to sleep was as peaceful as watching a sunset, and before I knew it, I fell fast asleep in his arms, our breaths, our heartbeats beautifully synchronized as one.

The next morning, I let Lucas sleep while I showered, slipped into my robe, then padded into the kitchen to prepare him breakfast. During his recovery, he had been limited to light meals like soup, toast, cereal, fruit, yogurt, in contrast to higher-calorie meals he'd been accustomed to eating, especially while strength training.

"Good morning." I tried to contain the wild smile on my face as I set the tray of food atop his nightstand.

"Morning," he said, sleepy gaze flicking from me, over to the tray. "You didn't have to make me breakfast."

I shrugged. "It's only a bowl of cereal, nothing fancy. How are you feeling?"

In one smooth move, he tugged me by the wrist, pulling me on top of him before flipping me onto my back. Of course, I giggled since it seemed Lucas Stone turned me back into a high school girl, giggling, blushing, wet-dreaming all day long.

Nudging my nose with his, he cupped my face with one hand, while his other hand settled on my waist, the contact giving me goose bumps. "I'm good, what about you?"

When he dragged his tongue over his lips, the memory of last night's kisses set desire ablaze in my belly. "I'm good."

He brushed my lips with his. "Doc was right, you know."

"About what?"

His lip curved up into a brazen smirk. "He told me if all best friends looked like you, one kiss wouldn't be enough."

"You better stop making me swoon." I bit his bottom lip.

"And how 'bout you stop making me want you." He tickled my waist with a squeeze, then glanced down at my robe. "Wait. Are you *naked* under this robe?" He let out a groan.

I nodded, mouth pressed in a hard line, willing myself not to giggle again.

"Fuck. It's cold shower time."

∾

THEY SAY time reveals all things.

Time with Lucas revealed—*proved*—my concerns about whether or not becoming more than friends would change the dynamic of our relationship were premature.

We still bantered. Still joked around. Still argued about who had the best dance moves. Only, as more than friends, we settled those playful grievances with hot make-out sessions, stopping ourselves when things started to overheat.

But, four days into his recovery, I was afraid my clit would jump out of my panties and tackle his mouth. I wanted sex with Lucas Stone. Badly. His hellafine ass and so-good smooches too impossible to resist.

Both combating our urges, we had to come up with ways to help win the no-sex-for-six-more-days battle. At night, we no longer slept in the same bed—actually, we'd squashed that right after our first night spent in his bed brought us a little too close to...well, coming —and during the day, we tried to focus on things that wouldn't make us think about sex. For me, that meant catching up on coursework, reading, and chatting with Chloe and Sage, while Lucas watched old game footage to spot areas he could improve upon, and caught up with friends like AJ, on FaceTime. Plus, there were showers. Lots of cold showers. And even though the days and nights spent not being able to share sexy times were brutal, pure torture, I relished in the thought that when he finally received the green light, Lucas and I would have hours upon hours full of explosive goodness.

"Can I take you on a date?" Lucas stood in the bathroom doorway, wearing jeans and a naked chest—*damn him*—chiseled lines of toned, too-good-to-be-real muscles on display. It was a little after 8 p.m., and he caught me as I was about to shower. I had plans to turn in early with Netflix and a bag of Doritos since I'd skipped dinner. Turned out early retreats to my bedroom were the only way to keep myself sane, keep me from jumping his bones.

"A date?" My cheeks heated, and I foolishly swiped them as if I could wipe the giddy surprise off my face.

"It's what couples do, right?"

"We're a couple?" I stammered, blinking up, trying to hold my gaze to his instead of the deep-set V I knew would make me salivate.

"Yes, silly." He hooked his index finger into the front pocket of my jeans, snagging me closer to him, my hands on his chest as he bracketed my waist. "What did you think we were, friends with benefits?"

Once again, warmth coated my face, and part of me wondered if I'd ever stop blushing whenever I was around him. "I'd love to go on a date with you. But, when? The first night after you're cleared?"

"No. We're going on a date tonight."

I stood there, thinking too much time in the house had made him lose his mind. He knew damn well it was against doctor's orders for him to go out, risk anything happening that would jeopardize his recovery.

I opened my mouth to counter, but closed it once he commanded my chin up with the light touch of his index finger, dazzling me with his stormy blues. "After you shower, I want you to put on an outfit you'd wear on a first date, then meet me in the kitchen in about an hour. I've ordered us Chinese takeout from that restaurant you're always talking about."

"Red Wok?"

He nodded. "That's the one. Now, hurry up and shower. You don't wanna be late for our date."

What can I say? He sure knew how to keep dousing me with that irresistible swoon magic.

After my shower, I quickly slipped into my favorite black maxi dress—slit on the side—and strappy high heels, my long hair in waves down my back. And to enhance my ensemble, I dabbed on a light coat of cherry-red lipstick, bringing out the coral-blue in my eyes, finishing it all off with a spritz of vanilla-scented perfume.

Like with any first date, butterflies bounced around in my stomach. Sure, Lucas and I had shared plenty of meals at some of the coolest restaurants—pizza, burgers, tacos—though none of those times were *date-worthy*, the sudden realization messing with my mind. What the fuck were Lucas and I supposed to talk about on our first date? We already knew everything about each other. Well, almost. Still, first dates were get-to-know-you dates, and the only thing I had yet to learn about Lucas Stone was how his naked body would feel on top of mine.

The click-clack of my heels seemed to be in tune with the pitter-patter in my chest as I rounded the hall.

Deep. Breaths. Macy.

Seconds later, I found Mr. Eye Candy in the kitchen, dressed in jeans, a chest-hugging button-down, dress shoes, and a dashing grin that made my heart, *and clit*, squeal in delight.

Mouth dropped, his gaze scrolled over me as he stood at the candlelit table with a single red rose in his hand. "Damn, Macy. You look so freaking beautiful."

"You're lookin' pretty damn hot yourself."

He chuckled, welcoming me at the table with a kiss on my cheek that, even in its most delicate form, left me breathless.

"This, of course, is for you," he said, handing me the flower.

It goes without saying, I gushed, practically melting in my own pile of fairytale-like bliss. "A single red rose, huh?"

He pulled out my chair. "Yep, and don't think I'm not aware of its significance."

We breezed through most of the delicious chicken fried rice and wonton soup meal with flirtatious small talk, before plunging deep into more personal topics.

"What Harper did to you, the cheating, it pretty much sucks. I didn't mean to minimize how awful that was by sort of laughing when you told me."

He stroked his jaw with the pad of his thumb. "You didn't minimize anything. Truth is, it was kind of funny, especially the look on her face when she got caught. What pissed me off was the time I'd wasted being with her when I could have, should have, been with you."

I swallowed, easing past the bubble in my throat, opting to stay silent, unsure of how to respond to that.

"No more talk about Harper. What's done is done, okay?"

I nodded, then took a sip of water, thinking I'd be better off pouring the cool liquid over my head.

"You and I already know so much about each other, but I'd like to talk about stuff we don't know. Is that all right?" he asked.

"Sounds good to me, although given we've known one another since we were kids, there shouldn't be too much left to discover."

We dabbled in relationship topics, like the number of kids we each wanted, career aspirations, questions about loyalty and honesty, only to discover we'd already known all those answers.

Lucas ladled more of the wonton soup into my bowl, then his. "Okay. Here's something I truly don't know about you. The other night you started to tell me who you were saving your virginity for back in high school. Mind telling me who?"

My stomach churned. I knew he'd come back to that eventually, and part of me also knew I would have done the same thing.

Letting out a deep breath, I spilled the tea like it was everybody's business. "Back then, I wasn't saving my v-card for anyone in particular. I was saving it for marriage."

"Marriage?" His brows climbed in surprise. "And, are you still saving it for then? For after you walk down the aisle?"

Lips pursed, I decided to toy with his mind. "Yes, absolutely no sex for me until my wedding night."

"Then we'd better book a trip to Vegas and get it done," he quipped, quick to not fall for my bullshit.

We were quiet for a few moments after that, studying each other as we finished off our soup. It felt good, even if nothing was said, his company more than enough.

"What we haven't talked about is sex."

I nearly choked on my slurp of soup.

"I want to know the number of guys you've slept with."

Caught off guard, I said, "If I tell you, will you tell me how many chicks you've been with?"

He knocked back a swig of water then nodded. "Yep. You go first."

"Two."

He scoffed. "Two? That's it?"

"Yes. Both in college—don't you dare ask who—and neither of them gave me an orgasm."

His lip curve was all cynical. "Okay. Two. And too bad about the orgasms, though I'm looking forward to giving you your first."

"Oh, I've had *plenty* of orgasms, thank you very much. All self-induced, but still," I huffed with a sense of woman-power pride. *Go me.*

"Right...it's not the same," he said, laughter in his voice. "I've jacked off plenty of times and, while it gets the job done, nothing compares to the real deal."

All that talk about sex and orgasms wasn't good for someone whose nights had been filled with a series of wet dreams. Looking to scurry off the subject, I said, "Okay. I spilled. Now it's your turn."

Head tilted to the side, he paused, eyes to the ceiling as if calculating the amount in his head. "Six. Which will make you lucky number seven."

Shifting, I crossed my legs, the uncalculated move exposing a bare thigh through the slit in my dress.

His eyes lingered on my thigh for beats unmeasurable before he pulled my chair closer to him, his index finger trailing up and down my thigh. The touch, electric, shot a wave of tingles throughout my spine, an instant message to the hankering between my thighs.

"In your confessions," he rasped, "you mentioned imagining you were a book heroine and I'm your book hero." Finger still caressing my thigh, he licked his lips. "Tell me, if this moment between us was written in a book, what happens next?"

I gulped.

Literally. Gulped. My dirty, horny little mind trapped in the gutter.

Breaths staggered, words became lodged in my throat, and when he slid off his chair to kneel at my legs, my whole body quivered.

"I know the kind of books you read, Macy." His voice was low, authoritative, and gruff, his eyes masked with desire. "They're hot, they're dirty, and if we were living out pages from *our* book, this is the scene where the hero tells the heroine to spread her thighs."

19

LUCAS

Waiting six more days wasn't going to happen, not when it came to tasting Macy Sinclair.

Blame how fucking hot she looked, or the smell of her perfume, or the way her thigh taunted me, seductively peeping out from beneath the slit of her dress, or blame the fact that being the first guy to give her an orgasm quickly became my greatest obsession. Doc's orders may have prohibited *me* from having sex, but there wasn't anyone who could tell me not to go down on the woman of my dreams.

On my knees, I pulled Macy's chair forward, her blue eyes dark, glazed with a combination of desire and apprehension.

"You trust me, right?" I eased her legs open, the high slit in her dress granting me a view that made my mouth and cock hungry.

She nodded, pulling her bottom lip between her teeth, hands gripped to the chair as if she were preparing for a wet and wild ride.

"Good to know." I ran my tongue along the inner part of her right thigh, ego-boosting satisfaction coursing through me when her breath visibly hitched. "Let me devour you, give you the orgasm you've been deprived of all these years."

She nodded again, rosy cheeks brandishing shyness while her mouth spewed nothing but confidence. "*Yes*. Orgasm. Please."

Gripping her waist, I tugged her lower body forward, allowing for easy access to fruit I'd once deemed forbidden, and I couldn't wait to take my first bite. Performing oral was my superpower, something perfected, mastered over time and while my lips and tongue were ready to dive in, I wanted to savor, explore, tease until I had her begging.

I slipped my hands beneath her dress, eager fingers finding sheer, black panties that had to come off. Sliding them down her legs, she sat there, breaths erratic, beautiful pussy exposed.

"Fuck, Macy," I whispered against her bare folds, "you're an effing goddess."

At the sound of her exhale, the corner of my lips curved up. I knew she was on the verge of panting even though the party had only just begun. I'd dreamed of taking her like this, watching her come against my tongue, the moment almost too surreal, I couldn't help but wonder if I was dreaming once more.

Squirming, Macy dug her fingers into my hair, tugging, making every attempt to guide me to her wet heat as my tongue brushed the inner part of her left thigh.

"Patience," I teased, tone commanding. "Good things come to those who wait."

"Shut up," she panted out; even while vulnerable with her legs spread wide over my shoulders, she was sassy as all hell. "I've been *waiting* for most of my life."

Running the pad of my thumb along her slick folds, I slid a finger inside her wet opening, taking pleasure in watching her eyes flutter closed. "So have I, baby."

I blew on her clit, and when her head fell back, I dove all the way in, taking my time, slowly licking, kissing, sucking and finger-fucking, my swollen cock on hind legs, begging for a piece of the action.

She tasted so good, so damn sweet, and it seemed the more I ate, the sweeter she tasted.

Her moans and whimpers were an erotic playlist to my ears, one I wanted on repeat for the rest of my life.

"Please, Lucas," she begged, hips grinding against my face. "*Please*, don't you ever...fucking...stop."

I had no plans to stop, increasing my lick, suck, and finger-fuck rhythm as she chased an orgasm, slowing my roll each time she was near.

"Tell me what you want, Macy." I flicked her clit. "Tell me what you *need* me to do."

High heels dug into my back, while her hands gripped the chair, salacious gaze pinned to mine. "*Come*. Please, Lucas. Make me come."

Going for gold, I moved my finger down, then up, taking her clit into my mouth again, circling it, massaging it with my tongue as she moaned.

Harder. *Softer*. Faster. *Slower*.

I played that methodical game over and over, each time leading her closer to the edge, until her body began to quake, the chair creaking beneath her.

"Oh, my fucking *Lucas!*"

Watching her unravel against my mouth was the sexiest shit I'd ever witnessed in my life. All I wanted to do was scoop her up, carry her into my bedroom, and feed her hungry pussy my cock for days. But the only action Mr. Dick would receive that night was a cold shower and a promissory note to get acquainted with Macy's sex pot the second after I was cleared to fuck.

Still kneeling, I helped my beautifully flustered Macy sit upright while she patted her hair into place, cheeks the color of bliss as she withdrew from her orgasmic high.

"Not bad for a first date, right?" I laid soft kisses along the slope of her neck.

"Dinner and an orgasm? Yeah, I can totally see that becoming the new dinner and a movie," she quipped, her razor-sharp wit on point. She snaked her arms around my neck. "Thank you for tonight, for being the first guy to give me pleasure."

I nudged her nose, one hand splayed along the small of her back, the other cupping her face. "The pleasure was all mine. You're amazing, sweet, addicting, and I want more of you." I grabbed her hand, guiding it to my throbbing cock that seemed to be looking for a way to escape the confines of my jeans. "See? I'm in need of a cold shower now." I pressed my forehead to hers, breathing her in, relishing the moment. "Thank goodness six days from now, cold showers will be a thing of the past."

"But, six more days feels like an eternity."

"No, baby." I sucked her bottom lip. "Not when you've waited as long as we have."

20

S hooting stars.

They're what I longed to see when I was younger, hoping to wish upon one that would make my biggest dream come true.

Back then, I had a crush on the boy next door, a dark-haired, blue-eyed, goofy-looking kid who, without reservation, invited me to play Bad Guy and Batman the day after my family moved into the house next to his. As we grew older, grew closer, he didn't seem to care that I wore braces, needed glasses for reading, or was a tomboy who wore pink, Converse high-tops or whether I donned pants or sparkly dresses. During that young and innocent stage in my life, other boys grossed me out.

But not him.

He made me laugh. Feel special. He made my whole world spin.

Each night before bed, I peered out my window, hopeful gaze on the hunt for shooting stars, never lucky enough to catch a glimpse. Instead, I closed my eyes and wished that Lucas Stone, the boy next door, would someday kiss me. Fast forward several adult years later, and not only did he kiss me, he *licked* me.

Between my thighs. Licks so motherfreaking good I saw thousands of shooting stars.

The next several days crawled by slower than a snail with asthma.

During his five-day post-concussion exam, Lucas was cleared for leisurely strolls around the block and everyday outings like trips to the market or visiting family and friends—so long as those visits didn't lead to strenuous activity. His MRI showed no signs of bleeding or damage, and since he'd never had a headache beyond the first day after the incident, the doctor told Lucas he could begin a light exercise routine supervised by team doctors. UCLA took head injuries seriously. Too many pro football players were diagnosed with a degenerative brain injury called chronic traumatic encephalopathy, or CTE. It was typically caused by repeated blows to the head, and most colleges adopted measures in taking extra precautions when it came to concussions. CTE had been something that worried me, lingered in the back of my mind ever since Lucas told me he wanted to go pro. I'd read heartbreaking news articles about how the disease affected football players young and old. The possibility of that happening to Lucas frightened me, and I had no problem voicing those concerns, even two days after his visit to the doctor while we were in the kitchen, cleaning up dishes after dinner.

"Hey," he said, commanding my chin up with his finger as always, "it's only one concussion, baby, a mild one at that. I promise you, I'm fine. I'll *always* be fine." His tranquil gaze bore reassurance into mine. "Besides, best news is doc said I'm cleared to fuck your sexy little ass in three more days."

Back against the kitchen counter, my lip curved into a coquettish smirk. "Oh? Too bad I'm on my period."

Bracketing my waist, he playfully rolled his eyes. "I know you're two weeks away from your monthly visitor."

Surprised, I said, "How do you know that?"

"Because I started tracking it four years ago when I noticed you get mad cravings for snacks one week a month. Without fail, you'd always ask me to run to the grocery store for dark chocolate, Cheetos, and Dr. Pepper. It's also the week you live in baggy sweats and a T-shirt, so I eventually put two and two together, added it to my calendar."

I blinked, a tad embarrassed.

"Anyway," he went on. "Ever notice how you no longer need to ask me to make those impromptu trips to the store? How your preferred munchies are already here for your taking?"

He waited for my sheepish nod before he continued.

"Well, that's because my calendar notifies me when to stock up on your snacks." He whipped his phone out of his jeans pocket, finger tapping the calendar app. "And according to this, I don't need to make a snack run for two more weeks." He showed me the recurring calendar entry labeled, *Buy Macy's Monthly Snacks*.

Warmth coated my heart, his thoughtfulness swaddling it like a blanket. Lucas Stone wasn't just boyfriend material, he was *book* boyfriend material, bits and pieces of perfect book heroes cut and pasted together, sprinkled all over the pages in the story of my life.

"That's probably the most generous thing anyone's ever done for me," I said, feeling kind of speechless.

"And here I thought that orgasm I gave you was the most generous thing anyone's ever done for you." He slid his phone back into his pocket, arms bracketing my waist once more.

"Well, I suppose it did satisfy a craving…"

He pulled me up against him and his obvious arousal, strong hands claiming my ass with a gentle squeeze. "I told you, your smart mouth does nothing but keep me hard."

"Then I'll be sure my mouth is a waterfall of sass when you're fucking me in three days."

~

"LOOK AT YOU, blushing like a virgin bride about to get shagged on her wedding night." Sage held up a zebra-print thong, lacy material dangling on the tip of her index finger. "What about this one?"

"Um, I don't think so," Chloe snapped, face screwed up like the Grinch. "The last thing she needs is for that zebra print to make Lucas dizzy, pass out, and reinjure his head all over again."

We were at The Bare Kitten because Sage and Chloe suggested I buy new lingerie. Lucas was a day away from being cleared for sex and, with the exception of some sexy lingerie, all of me was ready—dirty mind, waxed body, and sassy mouth.

"How about something simple?" I plucked a garment off the rack, holding it up for their approval. "Will this silk nightgown do?" After reading their disapproving faces, I snagged another. "Okay, what about this? It's comfy, cute, and considering it probably won't stay on me very long..."

"You're kidding, right?" Sage's hands met her hips. "We did *not* come here to buy a plain, white—albeit sheer—tank top for your fuckcute."

"My *fuckcute*?" I wanted to laugh out loud.

Sage crossed her arms over her chest. "As in, dick meets pussy for the first time?" she deadpanned.

"Right," I said, lips pressed in a hard line to quell laughter.

She sifted through more choices on the rack and said, "Anyway, you need to wear something memorable, as if your first time with Lucas is your wedding night. Lord knows you both have been waiting forever to consummate this relationship."

Her point was a valid one and I did feel like a bride-to-be preparing for her memorable wedding night.

"This!" Chloe held up the sexiest black, lacy bralette-and-panty set my eyes ever laid eyes on. Mesh. Lace. *Seductive*. Revealing in all the right places. "And look," she added. "The panty is basically crotchless for easy access."

The ensemble couldn't have been more stunningly perfect for me to wow Lucas.

"You need to try it on." Sage nudged me toward the fitting room, Chloe hot-footing it behind us. I'd expected them not to give me privacy, especially since I agreed to let them cast their vote of approval before my purchase.

Several minutes later, I stood in front of the mirror, completely taken by my own reflection. Usually self-conscious about my non-size-zero body, I'd never felt so sensuous, confident, *beautiful*. I knew I'd have no issue flaunting around half-naked in that ensemble, certain it would be an instant turn on for Lucas, which would be a guaranteed win for both of us. I wanted everything about our first night together to equal perfection. We owed it to ourselves, to each other, to our sexually deprived bodies.

Sage and Chloe rapped on the fitting-room door. "Let us see," they demanded in unison.

"You promised to get our approval before buying anything," whined Sage.

With a slide of the latch, I let the pestering crybabies in, both behind me as we all gawked at the reflection.

"Damn, woman." Chloe pursed her lips, head nodding in approval. "You're like, bow-down-bitch hot. Lucas is gonna bust both nuts just looking at you."

In need of her second approval to close the deal, I flicked my gaze to Sage's starry-eyed one. "So, what do you think?

"I'd totally do you."

21

LUCAS

"The dog-sitter canceled. *Canceled!* Less than four hours before we leave, no less." Mom's voice blared through my speakerphone, frantic. "But, Lola and Jack can't stay home alone for five days."

Mom and Dad—along with Macy's parents—went on a cruise to Mexico every year, something the four of them had done since we were in our late teens. Back then, Macy and I would babysit the spoiled pooches, camping out at my childhood home like we owned it. Occasionally we'd throw parties, but what teen didn't when their parents were out of town? Yet, it had been several years since we'd watched them. Mom hired Sally, a professional dog and house sitter, to take on the task. By the panic in my mother's voice, I supposed she wanted to know if Macy and I could hold down the pups while they were all gone.

"Want me and Macy to watch them?" I asked, already knowing the answer.

"Would you, hon? We have three hours to get to Long Beach or we'll miss embarkation."

Macy wasn't even back home yet. She had been out shopping with Sage and Chloe. Apparently she wanted to buy sexy lingerie for the next night—to commemorate my official clearance to have sex—even though I told her she'd look just as sexy in one of my T-shirts.

"Leave the key in the usual spot. Have fun on the cruise, Mom. See you all when you get back."

After ending the call with my mother, I texted Macy to let her know, figuring five days at my parents' six thousand square-foot home could be fun. Heated pool. Jacuzzi. It was one thing to enjoy those accommodations with Macy as a teen, even then her body, presence, hard to ignore. But being in a jacuzzi with Macy now?

Call me ruined.

Me: Hey, guess what happened?

I stared at the phone, in anticipation of her reply, relieved when I saw the text bubbles bounce on the screen.

Macy: Um, does it have to do with our parents' trip and Lola and Jack?

Me: Yes, how did you know?

Macy: My mom called me, completely unhinged, asking if we'd be up to watching Lola and Jack. Something about the dog-sitter bowing out?

Me: You okay with taking our party over there? I mean, we have plans...

Macy: As long as Jack doesn't try to hump me.

I laughed because, for whatever reason, Jack always humped Macy's leg as soon as she walked in the house.

Me: I'll be the only one humping you.

BETWEEN GETTING PACKED and ensuring our own house would be okay for five days, Macy and I didn't make it over to Mom and Dad's until after midnight. Lola and Jack went crazy, jumping all over us—*Jack trying to hump Macy's leg*—like they'd been alone for days instead of several hours.

While excited, eager, for what was to come, *literally*, we'd agreed, no matter what, to stick with our plans we made before jumping each other's bones—a romantic dinner at Befanos, a popular Italian restaurant, then back home, well, my parents' house, for fucking, lovemaking, and cuddles.

In that order.

I began to settle into the idea of spending the week together, playing house in luxury—a tiny glimpse into our possible future, me banking on money I'd earn in the NFL. I had plans to buy a large house and shower my woman, my family, with everything their hearts desired.

We set up camp in the guest bedroom since it was equipped with a king-size bed and sliding-door access to the pool and jacuzzi. My childhood bedroom wouldn't have worked since it pretty much looked the same as it was when I lived there with a full-sized bed that *I* barely fit into, let alone two people who probably needed as much space as possible when rolling around in the sheets.

I wanted Macy. Don't think it wasn't hard to fight every urge to skip the romantic evening planned and pound her, especially that morning when she pranced around the house in boy shorts and a tit-hugging tank top, her nipples screaming, *get over here and taste me*.

"Um, it's kind of hard to resist you when you're walking around here looking like *that*," I told her, slapping her ass as she sauntered past me.

She spun around, surveying me as she slurped coffee, a mischievous smile playing on her lips. "Likewise," she replied, "you, sexy, piece of man-candy tease."

I laughed; that sassy mouth never ceased to amaze me.

Dinner reservations were at 8 p.m. and with traffic being a

bitch anywhere in Los Angeles, Macy and I planned to head out at seven.

Showered and fully dressed in jeans, a silk tee, and socks until we were ready to leave, I fed Lucy and Jack, then let them run around in the part of the backyard cordoned off especially for them. The yard was a decent size, complete with an outdoor kitchen, a bar close to the pool, and a fireplace meant for snuggling. I used to catch my parents, snug, holding hands, exchanging kisses while sitting there, their golden relationship and beyond comfortable lifestyle, something to strive for. They'd met in college—Dad a football king, Mom a nerdy psychology major who tutored him on weekends. They were married before they graduated college, and soon after, Dad got drafted to play for the San Diego Chargers. Ten years later, I was born, my dad retired, and they moved to Beverly Hills, bought this house, and my mom set up her dream private psychology practice.

I'd always wanted their life. Love. Family. And, like my father, a successful NFL career with the monied lifestyle that so often accompanied it. But, despite what I told Macy because I wanted to protect her from further worry, the concussion did scare me. I mean, the game of football isn't hopping and skipping around in a meadow filled with birds and flowers. It's rough, brutal, and getting banged up on the field was par for the course. I could handle a busted kneecap, maybe even a broken leg. But CTE? Thanks, I'll pass. Thoughts of getting slammed into in a way that would lead to more concussions were unsettling.

Lucy and Jack yapped, yanking me out of my daze as I admired the view, soaking in the California sky as it changed from dusk to nightfall.

Glancing at my watch, I realized the time. I rounded up the barking brats, then decided to check in on Macy. I'd left her to get ready in the guest room with privacy to do whatever shit ladies did to prepare for dates. Already minutes before 7 p.m., I didn't want to risk us being late.

Ear to the door, I could hear music. Macy's voice singing along to the R&B track brought a smile to my face. Among other things, we had a love of music in common, both flexing in and out of genres with ease. Nothing fascinated me more than catching an unsuspecting glimpse of Macy while she danced around our house looking tantalizing as fuck, earbuds in place as she sang her favorite songs.

Knuckles to the door, I knocked.

Once. Twice. Three times. When she didn't answer, I twisted the knob to see if it was unlocked. It was.

Padding in, desire shot me straight in the cock.

Macy stood with her back to me, wearing nothing but a bra, panties, and please-fuck-me-tonight high heels.

Body swaying to the music, her smooth ass cheeks were on full display, a lacy-black thong hugging her perfect buns. Long hair that normally cascaded down her back, was pinned up, allowing my eyes to feast on the delicious contours of her back and a tiny pink-and-blue butterfly tattoo I had no fucking clue she had. The room was dim, save for the light spilling in from the en-suite bathroom. A black dress lay across the foot of the bed, and when she spun around to retrieve it, her eyes met my lustful ones. Of course, her front view presented more deliciousness than the back: an open-front bra that did very little to hide her perfect tits.

Macy Sinclair was a stunning piece of ass, and I wanted to officially make her mine, transport our relationship to the level it should have been years ago.

"Baby," I stammered, stupid mouth salivating. "I was just coming in to check on you. It's almost seven and…"

I stopped talking, lost in the fact she was too beautiful for words as she stood there, heat radiating from her eyes to mine.

Did she want me too? I hoped to God she did.

I ventured close, tentative, like a tiger stalking its next meal. Oh, wait. I *did* want her to be my next meal.

She padded toward me, cat-like stride in sync with mine. Her legs had always been drool-worthy, but perched in those heels? I was done. Heart stopped. Dead on arrival.

"I just need to slip into my dress," she said, her voice barely a whisper.

My cock jumped, or maybe it tried to sucker punch me, pissed off it was still inside my pants instead of deep inside Macy. "You look amazing, baby and, as you can probably tell, I can't take my eyes off of you right now, or ever."

We met halfway, the smell of her perfume like a match that set my raging testosterone on fire. Our bodies were flush, the chemistry explosive. Purposely, I refrained from touching her, aware that once my hands got a feel of her soft skin, the chemistry between us would be so combustable, I wouldn't be able to stop.

Her fingers crawled up and down the length of my chest, and part of me wished she'd stop. My throbbing cock became harder to control, a caged beast ready to be set free, ready to explore.

She bit down on her pillowy, gloss-coated lips. "Perhaps we can skip the fancy restaurant? Opt for an all-you-can-eat buffet instead?"

I dragged my gaze over her, admiring each curve, parts I hadn't yet tasted, the mesmerizing woman rocking every bit of my horny-as-hell world. "Five-star rated?"

She tugged at the hem of my shirt, our noses nudging, soft lips brushing mine. "Dress to impress, birthday suits required."

Mouth crashing down onto hers, my hands found her ample rump, and it goes without saying: all bets were right the fuck off.

"Get on the bed," I told her, suggesting she leave everything on, including those strappy heels.

As she sauntered over, I all but ripped my clothes off, stripping down to nothing but boxer briefs, boner proudly representing my last name, eyes glued to her, mouth panting as she climbed onto the bed. Music still played boom-boom base from the tracks, the perfect soundtrack for what we were about to do.

Macy welcomed me with open legs when I climbed onto the bed, our lips, our tongues reuniting, hips grinding, quick to discover their sensual groove as I lowered myself on top of her.

"Baby," I breathed out. "Even though we talked about it, I want to make sure you're on the pill—no condom, right?"

"Yes!" She raked her nails down my back. "Pill. No condom. Give me all of you."

Initiating my southbound journey, I licked the sensitive part of her neck, lingering until she tried, without success, to remove my boxers. "Didn't we talk about patience the other night? Trust me, baby." I unhooked the front clasp of her bra. "Taking our time will give us a generous payout."

Bra open, I admired her tits, perky nipples saluting me, my mouth sucking the right, then the left one, giving both handfuls the equal attention they deserved. She arched her back as I circled her nipple with my tongue, pulling the pebble between my teeth.

"Lucas," she hummed, "I swear, your mouth and tongue are so gifted, hitting me in all the right places."

"Wait until you meet my cock."

On a quest to get to know every inch, her body was like Mars, my tongue the Rover on an erogenous discovery mission.

Pausing at her stomach, I licked the area below the belly button, blowing, then gently grazing, aroused by the fact my barely-there touch erupted a trail of goose bumps along her skin.

"Please," she bucked her hips. "I...*need*...you."

I wandered back up to her lips, then whispered, "I know, baby. But, let me take my time and fuck you right, because tonight makes up for all the nights we've never had."

I n the game of football, Lucas Stone had several times been named MVP. Likewise, in the game of love and sex, he too was an MVP.

Most. Valuable. Pussylicker. He performed magical things with that mouth, giving me pleasure beyond my wildest fantasies, and I easily became addicted.

"Is this the lingerie you bought the other day?" He slid my panties off, tossing them onto the floor next to his boxer briefs. "Because if they are, note to self to buy you nothing but crotchless panties going forward."

All I could do was simper and nod, catatonically high from the Big-O his gifted mouth had bestowed upon me. Besides that, Lucas Stone was naked, perfectly manscaped, and the size of his wood standing at full attention made my mouth water. Let it be known, I'd never blown a cock before, but staring at the thick and lengthy work of art, well, I had a sudden urge to become Pornstar Penny.

Climbing out of bed, I got straight to my knees, grabbing his rock-hard party favor, taking it into my mouth like a pro.

He glanced down at me, his dropped jaw accompanied by a set of raised brows. "Macy, what are you doing?"

Or, maybe *not* like a pro, considering he felt the need to ask what I was doing.

Face hot as a furnace, I first felt embarrassed before growing quite offended. "I thought I'd give you oral...you know...like you've so selfishly given me." I ran my tongue along his shaft, then circled the tip, remembering it was something a book heroine did in one of many sexy-time scenes I'd read in a beautifully crafted Avery Flynn novel.

Head back, eyes closed, he growled, "*Fuck*, Macy," a reaction that quickly boosted my dwindling confidence.

When I was ready to take him into my mouth again, he stopped me. "Get up, baby."

I stood, high heels wobbly as I steadied myself, embarrassment charging back like a bull chasing red. Unsure of what to say, I bit down on my lip, gaze focused on his chest, careful to avoid his eyes.

"Hey." He raised my chin. "Look at me."

My eyes flicked to his.

"You don't know how many times I've fantasized about coming undone in your pretty mouth, these full, perfect-as-all-hell lips wrapped around my cock. But oral doesn't always have to be reciprocated." He ran the pad of his thumb along my sex. The only place I want my cock tonight, is deep inside of you."

I needed a slap in the face, *anything* to let me know I wasn't dreaming. "Pinch me so I know this is real, that *you're* real."

He chuckled. "Get back in bed, and I'll poke you instead."

I lay down, legs quivering, waiting for him to settle between them. I'd begun to feel nervous, butterflies wreaking havoc on my everything. Oral was one thing, but this? This was going to take our relationship to levels only in my dreams. They say sex can make or break a relationship, and while I had no doubts Lucas would be hot in bed, I was inexperienced in comparison, having more *controlled* sessions with my vibrator than the real deal.

He eased down beside me, rearranging the pillows as he sat up, back against the headboard. "I want you on top, riding me, taking me nice and slow."

That surprised me, turned me on, somehow settled my nerves, and quelled my fears of the unknown.

Doing as I was told, I climbed on top, straddling him, palms resting on his strong chest for support as our lips met tenderly.

My body quivered as his hands glided up and down my back until they settled on my bare ass.

Back arched, my fingers dove through his hair, hips grinding into him, my sex more than ready to accept him.

"Baby," he said, his teeth grazing my neck, "I can't wait anymore, I need to be inside of you."

"I thought we talked about the art of patience, Mr. Stone," I teased.

He slapped my ass cheek then squeezed it, his mouth sucking on my lower lip. "Ride me, Ms. Sassy."

Gaze locked on his hooded eyes, I rose up, letting him guide my hips down as I eased onto his thick cock, my breath hitching as he slid into me. God, he felt amazing as I rolled my hips, adjusting to his girth.

"*Fuuuck*, Macy," he growled. "You feel so damn tight, *so* damn good. So. Fucking. Good."

I rode him, up, down, rocking, rolling, as our kisses went from passionate to needy.

When I began to increase the pace, Lucas gently grabbed a hold of my hips and said, "Slow down, baby," his voice commanding yet hushed. "My cock wants to take its time getting acquainted with your sweet pussy."

There was something about the way he talked dirty to me that made me feel like his prized possession, his dominating tone alone capable of keeping me aroused. His hands traveled up to my hair, finding the pins to let my locks free, then he tugged, teeth nipping my neck, mouth roaming north until it found mine.

We kissed, slowly, lips and tongue in a synchronized rhythm with our lower bodies, as I alternated between rocking, riding, and grinding. I felt sensual, erotic, as though I could dissolve into him, the moment almost too much for me to handle.

I loved Lucas, and having him inside me felt right, and as meant to be as the moment I spilled my confessions for all to see. If not for that moment, I wouldn't be in his arms, with his lips devouring me, hearing him whisper, "That's right, baby. Nice and slow."

"*Lucas*." My head fell back, an insurmountable sensation building. "I'm close, baby," I breathed out. "Feels so good."

"Look at me, Macy," he demanded. "Look at me when you come."

Eyes fluttering open, I was taken when met with his lust-filled gaze, losing my mind when he circled my clit with the pad of his thumb.

I rode him fast, my body moving up, then slamming down onto his. "*Lucas*. Oh, *yes*. Baby, *yes*." Then faster, up, down, cupping my breast, chanting, *yes, yes, yes,* as he continued circling my clit.

Eyes locked, we stared, lost in the pleasure, lost in each other, mouths open, panting ravenously. I didn't want it to end, but at the same time, I wanted to give in to the orgasm my body so hungrily chased.

"Oh God, Lucas. I'm coming. I'm *coming*. Right...*now*." Body quaking, I rode out the glorious orgasm, collapsing into his chest, breathless, losing my strength to ride any further.

Lifting me off his lap, Lucas pulled out of me, flipping me onto my back, settling between my open legs.

He smiled greedily then licked my lips. "You look so hot when you come, *feel* so good around my cock when you come." He slid back inside me, my breath hitching once again at his girth. "Wrap your legs around me."

My legs went around him, my hands traveling up and down his back, occasionally cupping his ass as he pumped in and out of me.

He thrust deep, slowly circled his hips, then thrust again, continuing that feels-so-fucking-good pattern as his mouth sensually kissed all of me—my lips, my neck, my breasts, landing back on my lips for more.

He stopped thrusting for a minute, circling inside me as he stared into my eyes. "I love you so much, Macy. So. Freaking. Much."

As he kissed me, I melted into him, wanting again to be pinched, certain I was stuck in some stupid dream about one of those too-perfect book boyfriends. When his finger found my clit, I rocked against it as he began to thrust harder and faster.

I was going to come again. No doubt about it.

"Macy, I need you to come." He rubbed my clit. "Come all over my cock, baby."

And I did, so hard those shooting stars appeared again.

He followed after me, his cock pulsing inside of me as he met his release with another growl.

"Damn, baby." He kissed me. "Just...damn."

It's how I felt, too, and like that, Lucas went from Most Valuable Pussylicker to Most Valuable Penis in twenty minutes flat.

And I was lovestruck—*cockstruck*—for life.

"WE SHOULD PROBABLY ORDER something to eat since we skipped dinner." Lucas wrapped a towel around me as we stepped out of the shower.

It was close to 10 p.m. and after three rounds of sex, including one round in the shower, I'll admit I could have eaten an entire supermarket.

"Why don't we cook something instead?" I suggested. "Your parents always have a stocked fridge and considering they were expecting the house sitter, I'm sure there's something we can whip up in a flash."

"Okay, but put this on." He gave me the silk tee he never got to wear to dinner. "I've always wanted you in one of my shirts."

Inside the kitchen, Lola and Jack hung out with us as we prepared a batch of pancakes, our favorite go-to late-night meal. The kitchen was huge; in fact, the whole house was larger than the house I grew up in. And seeing I had spent more time at Lucas's house than my own, I knew my way around his pretty well.

Before they retired, my parents were gone from home a lot— Dad on movie sets and Mom working on news stories. Both sets of grandparents lived out of state, visiting only for holidays. I found myself over at Lucas's often, even spending the night if my parents were out of town. Their absence is probably what made Lucas and I close, our bond thicker than blood.

"Remember that night we got into a huge fight over Calvin Markes?" Lucas scooped pancake batter onto the griddle, the pan sizzling.

I snorted out a laugh, slicing pieces of a banana. "Yeah, how can I forget? You found out I'd asked him to Sadie Hawkins, then you basically went ballistic."

"Well, I wouldn't call it ballistic..."

"Really? Because looking back, I'm pretty sure you all but lifted your leg, pissed, and marked your territory." I shook my head, smiling at the memory. "I mean, we were barely in middle school and already you didn't want any of your friends near me."

He flipped a pancake. "Proof I've been loving you for a long time but too afraid to admit it." He added the final pancake to a tall stack on the plate, then walked over to me, snaking his arms around my waist from behind. "We didn't speak for days and it was then the realization of having you in my life, even if only as a friend, was better than not having you at all."

I felt the warmth of his breath skating across the nape of my neck, flames extinguished after our shower flickering back to life. I placed the knife down, then spun around to face him, palms skating across the contours of his bare chest. "And that's when we made the pact to forever and always remain best friends."

Beats of silence rolled by as his gaze held mine captive, the reflection from the ceiling lights sparkling in his blue eyes, showcasing their mesmerizing, hypnotic hue.

He rested his forehead against mine, hands cupping my face. "Stupid pact, the one I wanted to kick in the balls by the time we got to high school."

"Me too, but even more during rush week when I saw you run across the field naked." I grabbed his ass. "One look at this, and I was swooning for days."

His head fell back in a chortle. "You saw *that*?"

"Yep. And I've been a bona-fide hot mess over you ever since."

He nudged my nose. "I'm sorry we waited so long to get here. But now that I have you, I'm never letting you go."

"You promise?"

"Promise. I'm yours forever."

ACT TWO

"If you never chase your dreams, you will never catch them."

23

LUCAS

hree Months LATER

"I miss you already." I blew Macy a kiss through the screen on my phone as AJ and I snaked through the crowd at Indianapolis International Airport. "I'll call you tonight before I go to sleep. And baby"—I paused, waiting until FAA announcements stopped blaring through the airport speakers—"I love you."

It was February, the week of the NFL Combine, a pre-draft event hundreds of the best college football players were invited to. Everyone from coaches, scouts, team executives, and medical staff, from thirty-two NFL teams, were expected to be there, evaluating top college football players eligible for the upcoming draft. It was like an intense job interview for athletes who were chasing dreams of playing in the NFL, complete with panel interviews, medical exams, and agility tests.

"You gonna be able to breathe without her, man?" AJ slapped my back. "It's like a nonstop love fest with you two. Sage and I don't even do that 'bye, I love you' shit anymore."

"That's 'cause you and Sage are too busy being on again and off again to find your love groove."

"Oh, we've found our groove. Right between the sheets, where it matters most."

Outside, the winter air bit my face, a flurry of snow cascading from the sky, lightly coating the ground. I loved the cold contrast from Los Angeles where it was in the low seventies when I left.

Inside the Uber, our drive from the airport wasn't too long as we made our way downtown, tall buildings, restaurants, bars, and shops surrounding us. To the left of us, at the stoplight, was Lucas Oil Stadium, home of the Indianapolis Colts and the NFL Combine adjacent from our hotel.

"Can you believe I just now noticed the stadium is named *Lucas* Oil?" AJ's voice wobbled with laughter. "That's some funny shit."

I snapped a photo of the stadium's facade, firing it off to my baby in a text, a smile tilting my lips. "Yep. It's all Macy's been teasing me about this whole week."

He looked at me, head shaking after his assessment. "Dude, you have it *bad* for her. Worse than I thought."

I slipped my phone into my coat pocket, then opened the car door as the driver pulled up to our hotel. "Tell me about it."

There was no point in denying how I felt about Macy. The past three months, plus all the milestone first holidays as a couple— Thanksgiving, Christmas, New Years, Valentine's Day—only drew us closer, more intimate, our sex life, the impromptu blow jobs she gave, hotter than the sun. Our circle of friends, family, both sets of parents, loved us as a couple, all citing they'd figured we'd someday end up together, our chemistry too crazy-hot to remain just best friends. I had plans for me and her—ones that included us walking down the aisle and starting a family. I wasn't the type of guy who sought out to avoid marriage. Raised to value the love of a good woman and the sanctity of matrimony, it had always been on the top of my things-to-do list, right beside getting drafted by the NFL.

After we checked in at our hotel, AJ and I made it up to our suite, stopping to talk to players from teams in our division.

"Dang, this room is *legit*." AJ tossed his duffel bag onto the couch, then plopped down beside it, feet resting on top of the table in front of it. He surveyed the suite, head bobbing in approval. "Kinda feels like they're giving us a fine taste of rookie life."

He had a valid point.

Our two-room suite at the Crowne Plaza turned out to be pretty dope, complete with all the amenities, plus a few extra bells and whistles, courtesy of the Combine sponsor who, that year, happened to be Verizon. The five-day event was expected to be action-packed, beginning the day of our arrival. Tight ends, wide receivers, and quarterbacks were on the same tier, attending and participating in events together, which is why AJ and I were able to travel together and share a suite. His football aspirations mirrored mine, and we hoped to be drafted to the same pro team, carrying our winning legacy with us into the NFL.

My eyes perused the schedule handed to me at check-in. "Bro, we need to head down for registration and orientation."

BEING NAMED one of college football's best players came with an influx of media attention at Combine. Sure, I'd been somewhat prepped for media and the frenzy they toted, giving countless postgame interviews whenever ESPN covered UCLA games.

But holy, shit.

Stepping out of the orientation room, the convention center lobby was definitely a media circus. Reporter after reporter stopped me, asking me what pro teams I was talking to and if I'd had talks to sign with Nike, Adidas, or Under Armour, the real-deal possibilities, equally overwhelming and euphoric.

"Is it true Dallas has their eyes on you?" A smug-as-hell reporter from Sports Illustrated rocked back on his feet.

I took a sip of Perrier, a smirk tilting the corner of my mouth. "I've learned to steer clear of rumors and let chips fall where they may come Draft Day."

"You seem a bit overconfident," said the same reporter. "What if, as an expected first-round pick, you get drafted by one of the NFL's worst teams?"

I remembered the same reporter had been a dick at Rose Bowl the year before. "My father once told me to never waste time in the crazy land of *what-ifs*."

ONCE I GOT through orientation and the burn from media questions, my first day was wrapped up with one of several team interviews to take place throughout the week, two of which were to be one on one with team coaches and executives.

After grabbing dinner provided to us at the hotel, AJ decided he wanted to hang out at Nike's accommodation suite for a few hours, while I chose to head straight to our suite, wanting nothing more than a shower and a phone call to my girl.

"How was your first day?" Macy's eyes sparkled through the phone, her face beaming. "They played a clip of your media interview on ESPN. You are officially a hometown quarterback hero."

I propped my head on the pillows. "Yeah, and that prick reporter wins the Dicky Bitch Reporter of the Decade award. Other than that, my first day went well, though I'm pretty exhausted. How are you?"

She sighed. "I'm fine, just studying. I want to hurry up and graduate already."

"I miss you, baby. Wish you were here, curled up next to me. You should have come with me, got your schoolwork done while I was at all-day events. Plus, you could be in the stands, watching me do agility tests and drills on Thursday."

"You know very well why we agreed I shouldn't join you. This week you need to be completely focused on all things football and get plenty of rest at night, not being distracted by my hot ass."

Though she meant to be funny, it was true. No matter how much I wanted Macy with me, it was best she stayed behind. Lying next to her at night, there would be no rest because even three months after our first fuck, I still couldn't seem to get enough of her.

"What's tomorrow look like?" She took a sip of Red Bull.

I explained I'd have a hospital pre-exam, interviews, and that I'd likely visit the Nike suite to get a massage.

Her brows lifted. "A massage? Do I need to be worried about you getting tempted by football groupies looking to score a guy with a potential fat check?"

"Stop." I chuckled, confident she wasn't the jealous type, especially since I never gave her a reason to be. "You know you're the only one who will ever score with this guy."

THE NEXT FEW days went by in a flash.

Medical exams, the big Wonderlic test filled with problem-solving questions to measure how quickly I answered the questions correctly—of course I passed with a high score—NFL union meetings, followed by the insanely brutal team-coach interview.

Strutting into the interview was like walking into an inquiry in front of a judiciary committee. They all sat behind a table with microphones while I sat at a podium, nothing but a glass of water at my disposal.

Like strategic missiles, questions were fired at me left and right.

"Do you think the NFL owes you a career because your father had a successful pro football career?" the coach from Dallas asked without a flinch.

Now, keep in mind it was expected they'd ask tough questions designed to garner a reaction out of me. Mainly because they wanted to put feelers out, test my integrity, gauge how I reacted under pressure.

My jaw ticked, the one-year stint on the high school debate team my dad encouraged me to participate in, finally paying off. "The NFL doesn't owe me anything, but, *I* owe the NFL my dedication, athletic agility, and crazy love of the game."

More questions were thrown at me, some of which were on-the-field related where I was asked to draw a diagram of a strategically thought-out winning play.

The interview lasted about eighteen minutes and most of the questions—as brutal and thought-provoking as they were—rolled off me like water.

Until the last one.

"Given the nature of the sport, what if the prospect of receiving a diagnosis of CTE is deemed unavoidable?"

Jerk-off.

Of course, he asked that, probably all-too-familiar with my one and only concussion.

Life and everyone important to me flashed before my eyes—friends, family, *Macy*—along with thoughts that I would never want to put them through the pain of watching me suffer from a critical brain disease.

Coaches from five of my most influential teams—Dallas, New York, San Francisco, Atlanta, and New England—surveyed me, their expressionless faces taunting.

Stomach tightening, I internally prayed the only answer in me didn't ruin my chance at getting drafted by one of the teams in the room. "While I tend not to get bogged down by useless *what-if* scenarios, the answer to your question is, simply put, I wouldn't play the game."

24

MACY

"**O**n a scale from one to ten, this is bad. *Real* bad." Sage squatted over the toilet as she aimed for the stick. "I *can't* be prego."

Three weeks after Lucas and AJ's return from their trip to the NFL Combine, Sage sat in the bathroom, looking like her mixed-up cat named Pooch just died, admitting she and AJ had failed to use a condom the night he got back home.

"I mean," she sobbed, "he did that blow on my clit magic, and next thing I knew, we were going at it on his living room floor, no condom, the asshole claiming it felt too good to pull out."

I rubbed her back, hoping to console the wave of emotions. "Well, that magical blow is known to set things on fire. When Lucas does that, it gets me every single time."

Chloe hopped onto the bathroom counter, arms folded over her chest. "I sure wish someone would blow on my clit."

Sage and I shot her a look, and I bit my lip to quell any morsel of laughter.

"Well," I began, "if you stop freaking out whenever it's time to get down and dirty, maybe someone will blow on *all* of your sacred lady parts."

Fact of the matter, Chloe was a closet virgin, too afraid a guy would run for the hills if he found out she'd never gone farther than second base. We had tried convincing her several times that some guys would give their left nut to score a hot virgin.

"When is it supposed to change color?" Sage placed her test stick on the counter beside Chloe, then stepped over to the sink to wash her hands.

"Five minutes," I said matter-of-factly.

Chloe and Sage narrowed their eyes at me suspiciously.

"What?" I scoffed. "Lucas and I had a week of uncertainty before Christmas. Since then, it's been Condom City—*most times* —even though I'm on the pill."

"Geez, Macy," Chloe said. "What would you have done if your test ended up positive?"

Truth was, the thought of having a baby excited us both. We picked out names and were disappointed when we learned my cycle had just shifted. But with graduation around the corner, I wanted to focus on applying to magazines, get ready to launch my journalism career the way Lucas had started to launch his NFL career. Only two weeks before the draft, things were likely about to significantly change for him. I just hoped things wouldn't change significantly between us. Playing with the big guys was a whole new level. Travel seemed more intense, as was the time at practice, not to mention the game tended to be even rougher, the risk of injury tripled. And don't get me started on all the women— beautiful women who throw themselves at rookies days after signing contracts. I wish I hadn't read that most existing relation- ships suffer once college players go pro.

"It was exciting to imagine having his baby, and someday I'm sure we will have one," I told them. "Now, let's wait and see what this stick says before we start planning Sage and AJ's shotgun wedding."

Five minutes always seemed to slowly tick-tock by when clock-watching, and as soon as the timer went off, Sage and Chloe both reached for the test.

In what felt like slow motion, the stick flew out of one—maybe both—of their hands. My ears hurt listening to them squeal as the test soared into the air. Sage tried to catch it but failed miserably as it sailed, performing acrobatic twists and turns, until it finally landed facedown on the floor. Instead of reaching down to pick the test up, we all stood there gawking, jaws dropped, hands slapped to our faces like the kid in Home Alone.

Pooch trotted in, scooped the test into his mouth then dashed off, presumably for the cat door-flap thing that provided him an escape route outside.

"*Fuck!*" Sage yelped, charging after him. "Crazy cat's gonna bury my kid-is-in-the-oven stick."

"Wait," Chloe said as we both ran after her. "You got to see how many lines it had before it fell?"

Sage stopped in her tracks, collapsing onto the couch as she gave up on being able to catch Pooch. "Yep." She ran her fingers through her hair. "Pretty sure there were two lines on that little fucker."

～

"PREGNANT?" Lucas toyed with my hair. "Maybe a baby will make them get their shit together."

I ran my hand along his sculpted abs as we lay nestled in bed, my head resting on his chest, the boom-boom rhythm of his heart soothing. We'd just had a round of sex and were riding our post-orgasm high. Sexy times with him only got better and better, our love for each other, our bond seemingly unbreakable.

"Remember when we had our pregnancy scare?" I asked, the memory of it all more vivid since the topic came up when I was at Sage and Chloe's house.

He kissed my head, running his fingers along my arm, his touch forever spine-tingling. "It wasn't a scare, not for me anyway. I remember hoping you were so we could fast-track and get married."

"Married?" I blinked up at him. "Marriage is something we've never really talked about."

"Didn't think there was a need to, considering you've talked about wanting a fairy-tale marriage ever since you were a kid. I just figured that much hadn't changed."

I giggled internally, appreciating how he paid so much attention to me growing up. "True, but we haven't talked about how *you* feel about marriage in general and not when a couple thinks it's the right thing to do because a baby is on the way." My heart stopped, thinking back to his short-lived engagement. "Why did you propose to Harper?"

He exhaled, a tad dramatically in my opinion. "We agreed to never talk about her again, remember?"

"Sure, but I'd still like to know what made you propose to her since you clearly didn't love her." *Or so you claimed.*

"Macy," he warned, "I don't wanna talk about this."

I shot up, quickly pulling the sheet up over my exposed breast, not giving his gaze a chance to devour them. "You know how much I hate when you put your avoidance hat on." Although in his defense, he'd not avoided much lately, or maybe I hadn't presented him with anything he deemed worth avoiding.

"Macy..." he warned yet again, voice and eyebrows raised.

"Tell me why you proposed," I demanded.

"Seriously? You think I wanna talk about another chick while I'm in bed with you?" The clipped tone of his voice irritated me.

I climbed out of bed, slipped into his T-shirt, then walked around to his side, arms crossed over my chest. "I'm not in bed with you anymore, so go ahead. Spill it, Mr. *Avoidance*." I swallowed the lump of emotion crawling up my throat, hating that it seemed like we were on the verge of our first couple fight. Regardless, I charged on like a shark that just got a whiff of fresh blood. "Why did you propose to Harper if you were supposedly in love with me?" It was a question I never knew I wanted the answer to until the moment it consumed me.

Silence choked the room, save for our collective breathing, tension between us palpable.

Lucas got to his feet, slipped into his shorts, and shouldered past me when he said, "Not tonight, Macy."

Not tonight, Macy? Ugh. Wrong. Answer.

I stalked after him as he rounded the corner and made his way into the kitchen, muscles in his back flexing. God, the fact he looked so damn yummy to my eyes, even when I was pissed off at him, was beyond annoying.

"Lucas, why are you making this such a big fucking deal? Just tell me why you asked Harper to marry you."

He swung the fridge open, then immediately slammed it closed, feet pounding the floor as he advanced toward me.

For every step forward he made, I stepped backward, until my back kissed the cool kitchen wall.

Eyes the color of anger bore down on mine as our bodies stood flush, our breathing crazy-fast, and I swear my heart ran for cover, skidding down to my stomach for safe refuge.

Determined to know, I said once more, "Tell me why," waiting with bated breath, watching his jaw tick, the vein in his neck pulse.

He grabbed the nape of my neck, drawing me so close I thought he'd swallow me whole.

"Because," he rasped. "I had to get the fuck away from you."

25

LUCAS

trengths. Weaknesses.

We all have them. Some more or less than others. Lucky for me, my strengths—loyalty, patience, self-control —outweighed my biggest weakness: avoiding conflict.

Years back, I had categorized my weakness as a strength, often boasting that I rarely had arguments, fights, or disagreements, and most women appreciated that about me.

But, Macy? *God, Macy.* She always pushed, digging her questions into me like a blade, jabbing and prodding until I bled nothing but answers.

Contrary to what she may have assumed, believed, or guessed, my propensity to lean toward avoidance wasn't always for my benefit alone. Sure, there were instances where I needed time to process, take in, and figure shit out on my own. Yet, many times, avoidance supplied me with comfort in knowing, in the heat of any given moment, I wouldn't say something stupid that would inevitably end up hurting her feelings. Seeing Macy hurt fucked with me—and in that sense, maybe avoidance was a form of self-protection.

I knew the burning question regarding why I proposed to

Harper would fire up eventually. Perhaps I should have chosen to proactively clear the air, provide her the TMI rundown. At the same time, part of me was ashamed that I'd asked a woman I didn't love to marry me, simply to avoid the woman I was crazy in love with.

A word to the wise: Don't be stupid.

I had to get the fuck away from you.

Thinking back, that wasn't the best delivery, not when her voice was already shaky, eyes on the verge of spilling tears.

"Yeah? Well, Lucas Stone, let me make that easy for you."

She pushed past me, ponytail swaying back and forth as she stomped off. I should have gone after her but didn't because, *hello*, conflict-avoiding jerk here. Before long, I heard the front door slam shut, the sound of her shoes hitting the pavement, and seconds later the sound of her car starting.

Way to go, asshole.

I woke up in a panic, hand reaching over to Macy's side of the bed, only to find her gone.

Still.

I got out of bed to check in what was once her bedroom before we became a couple. Flicking on the light, I was met with nothing but an empty guest bed and the desk she used when blogging, which she didn't do much of ever since bloggergate.

Hours had passed since she stormed out, phone calls and texts left unanswered.

I'd given her some reason to be angry with me, but I wasn't really sure why nor did I expect her to become the avoidant.

Back inside our room, I climbed back in bed, then checked my phone.

Nothing.

The time showed 2 a.m. *Where the fuck is she?*

Worry impaled my throat, making it difficult to swallow past the anger I had toward myself for being the world's biggest idiot. It was all my fault and I wanted to fix it.

I fired off what felt like text number one billion fifty-seven.

Me: Baby, please come home, or at least let me know you're safe.

Her reply whooshed in instantly.

Macy: I'm safe.

Me: Where are you?

It took about five excruciating minutes for her response to stroll in.

Macy: Everywhere you're not.

Damn, when pissed off, she sure had one hell of a bite.

Not wanting to push any further I sent a simple reply.

Me: Glad you're safe. I love you.

Of course, she never replied.

~

"I'm FREAKING OUT, DUDE." AJ paced my living room floor, bags under his eyes, hair wild like Einstein. "Me? A dad? No fucking way."

I sat on the couch, eyes tracking his movement from left to right, and I started to feel seasick. "You're one-hundred percent sure she's pregnant?"

He plopped onto the recliner, elbows on his knees as he raked his fingers through his messy hair. "Pooch took off with the stick and buried it before she had a chance to confirm the results. But, she's two weeks late with sore tits, fatigue, and of all things"—he rose to his feet and started pacing again—"she suddenly can't stand the smell of my cologne. Five bottles of that shit sitting on my bathroom counter and now I can't even wear one drop without her heaving."

"Well, in all fairness, the smell of your cologne kind of makes *me* wanna heave, too."

He stopped pacing long enough to pin a glare on me. "Fuck you, Stone."

I coughed into my fist to hide my chuckle and watched him continue to pace, hoping the back and forth trek would quell what looked like a panic attack waiting to happen.

"What are you gonna do?" I asked even though the answer was etched into his face. AJ loved Sage, despite their on again, off again issues. High school sweethearts, they came to UCLA together all the way from a small town in Nebraska. There was no way he'd abandon her to figure it out on her own. Their bond was stronger than superglue. The thought made me think of the bond Macy and I had as best friends. I hoped to God our bond as a couple would prove to be equally strong.

AJ parked back down onto the recliner and breathed, "I love the shit out of her, man. Always have. Always will." He leaned back, a sense of calm settling into his eyes. "I think I'm gonna marry her."

I couldn't help but think about Macy, badly missing her since our blowout the night before. Plucking my phone off the coffee table, I sent her a text.

Me: Hey, come back home.

26

MACY

For most, there's no place like home. For me, there's no place like home when pissed off at your boyfriend.

Normally, to nurse my wounds, I would have ended up sprawled across the couch at Sage and Chloe's place, glass of wine in one hand, slice of pizza in the other. But honestly, I didn't want them to know there was trouble brewing in my paradise, didn't want to sit and explain how I took off in a foot-stomping fury, instead of sharing my root issues. Plus, Sage had enough on her plate with the assumed pregnancy.

So, I drove straight home to Mom and Dad's. Then crept upstairs to my bedroom, complete with its hot-pink curtains and NSYNC posters thumbtacked to the walls, crashing facedown onto my bed, then cried. Cried and cried. I ignored most of Lucas's texts, afraid he'd charm me into coming back home. Hurt, confused, angry, I needed space, time away from the man who lovingly held my heart in his hands and, at the same time, squeezed it.

Mom and Dad didn't even know I'd come home until the next morning when I padded downstairs to hush my growling belly.

Thank goodness they were both fully dressed instead of like

that one unseeable time when I'd walked in on them conducting old-married-folk business—*doing it*—on the family room sofa— *gross, because they're my parents, okay*—doggy style.

Needless to say, I made a point to never sit on that sofa again.

Mom's face brightened like the moon in a desert night sky. "Macy Cake! What in the world are you doing home, sweetheart?"

Macy Cake had been my nickname since I was about two years old. As the story's been told, too many times to count, after my mom presented a cake at my birthday party with "Here's Macy's Cake" I proceeded to call every cake I laid eyes on after that a Macy Cake.

Dad peered up at me from the newspaper he was reading, black-rimmed reading glasses the same style as mine. "Hey, baby girl. When did you come in?"

Mom and Dad.

If they had a slogan that defined them as a parental brand it would say, "Conservative Facade. Hippies at Heart."

Working hard to give me an amazing upbringing, their jobs often kept them from home more than I would have liked. They were older and had me in their late forties, one of the reasons why I had been an only child. Retiring soon after I graduated high school, they'd spent ample time making up minutes, seconds, hours of lost time with me growing up.

After I gave them both a kiss on the cheek, Mom must have assessed a look on my face, the one I'd tried to hide with a grin.

"What happened?" she asked, thumb grazing my chin, forcing me to look up and into her eyes. "You and Lucas have a falling out?"

Dad cleared his throat, tossing his newspaper onto the table. "Now, you know I love Lucas like a son. But, if I need to whip his ass, you just tell me when and where."

Mom grabbed my shoulders, guiding me to the kitchen table. "Sit, Macy Cake. I'll make you some breakfast and then we'll talk."

Once breakfast was devoured, Mom prepared me a cup of her famous cinnamon-stick coffee. My phone sat on the table and buzzed with a text message from Lucas.

Lucas: Hey, come home.

I rolled my eyes even though my heart warmed, imagining how his voice would sound saying the words in his text message. He'd hum them with his seductively commanding timbre. The fact was, it had been less than twenty-four hours since our spat, and there I was...missing him.

Mom settled down in the seat beside me with that knowing gaze all mothers were gifted with. "What happened?"

Hesitation stung my tongue at first, then after a sip of Mom's coffee, I remembered she had a tendency to make everything better.

"Getting Lucas to open up, refrain from avoiding certain topics, is like pulling teeth from a pair of bears on a stroll with their cubs."

"He's a guy. It's sort of what they do." She slid one of her knowing looks over to my dad. "Right, honey?"

"I have no idea what you're talking about," he deadpanned.

Mom chuckled. "Case in point."

Explaining everything in detail, I held nothing back, including his words before I stormed off, head on fire.

I needed to get the fuck away from you. Nine words no one should live by.

"What do you think he meant by that?" Dad asked, stroking the gray stubble on his jaw.

I shrugged, willing stupid emotions not to get lodged in my throat. "All I know is he would have married Harper if I didn't accidentally mic-drop my digital diary online."

That factoid is what shattered me the most, thoughts of him just letting me get away—him *getting the fuck away from me*—without a fight.

"If it were me he was in love with," I went on, "why not take a chance and tell me instead of giving a ring to someone else?"

Mom sighed, reaching over to tuck a loose strand of hair behind my ear. "Honey, if you want to know the answers to those questions you need to ask Lucas yourself."

She wrapped her arm around my shoulder, and I squeezed my eyes shut, readily leaning into her embrace.

"Can I stay for a while? I'm not quite ready to go home yet."

Mom rubbed my shoulder, kissed my forehead, then said, "Stay as long as you want, Macy Cake."

LATER ON WHILE up in my room, I took advantage of time away from Lucas to catch up on finals pre-work. Additionally, I updated my resume, submitting it to magazines all over the country in hopes to get called in for an interview. Letting the opportunity with *Hot Shot* float by haunted me. I'd probably never be offered an opportunity as good as that again.

Regardless, I needed to find work after graduation. *Redbook*, *Maxim*, *AllYou*, *Cosmopolitan*, and *Allure*, were all the places I'd applied to, fingers crossed for some type of post-grad internship or, better yet, a job offer.

In need of a snack, I headed down to the kitchen, catching a glimpse of my parents cuddled up on the family room couch, munching on popcorn while watching Iron Man. Relief washed over me, thankful I hadn't caught them getting down and dirty.

"Grab yourself some popcorn and join us," Dad insisted, mouth full of popcorn.

For Christmas, they'd purchased themselves one of those old-fashioned popcorn machines that sits on a stand. Hands down, it made the best-tasting popcorn, like the kind you'd get only at the movies. I grabbed a bowl, scooped up some of the buttery goodness, then took a seat on the smaller couch, cringing at first, praying they'd never had sex on that one too. I never passed on a chance to watch Iron Man, watching it over ten times with Lucas, each instance discovering some little tidbit I'd missed before.

The doorbell rang, and my dad padded over to answer it, leaving Mom to gush, cheeks tomato red over Robert Downey, Jr.

Beats later, Dad said, "Macy Cake? Look who's here to see you."

I turned around, nearly dropping my bowl of popcorn.

My stupid heart squealed, jumping up and down like a cheerleader in my chest, cheering, *Yes, he's here! I said, yes, yes, he's here.*

Lucas stood, dressed in a white form-fitting T-shirt, basketball shorts, flip-flops, and a UCLA ball cap positioned backward, atop his head. Missing him, he definitely was a site for sore eyes and heart to see.

He rocked back on his heels, flashing that half smile I could never tire of. "Hey."

27

LUCAS

Waiting for her to come home got old pretty quickly, and when Sage told me Macy wasn't at her apartment, I knew she'd gone home to her parents.

"Honey," said, Paul, Macy's dad. "We can stream Iron Man upstairs."

Beverly, her mom, kissed me on the cheek, and Paul patted me on the shoulder before they grabbed their bowl of popcorn and walked hand in hand up the stairs, leaving me alone with their daughter. Her parents had always liked me, trusted me since the first time I'd rung their doorbell and asked if their little girl could come outside and play Bad Guy and Batman with me. Only six years old, I never would have guessed that many moons later, I'd end up falling for the blonde girl with uneven pigtails, bright red cheeks, and sparkly dresses.

She sat still as a statue on the couch, eyes focused straight ahead to the TV, as I eased down beside her, my thigh grazing hers.

"Missed you," I said, my voice low, subdued, elbows pinned to my thighs, hands in a steeple.

She offered me some of her popcorn, eyes still glued to the scene on the large TV screen, clearly willing her eyes not to take one glance over at me.

A cloud of awkwardness hovered above us, and I desperately wanted to find its kill switch.

"Baby"—I cleared my throat—"I'm really sorry about last night."

Macy leaned over to the rectangular coffee table, placed the popcorn down, then flicked the TV off with the remote. As she turned around to face me, legs tucked under her yoga-style, remorse filled my chest. I could tell by the puffiness in her eyes she'd been crying—which meant I'd hurt her, the last thing I wanted to do.

"What did you mean when you said you needed to get the fuck away from me?" Her voice wobbled as though a flurry of emotions were stuck in her throat.

Fear sliced my heart in two, afraid my stupid mouth would inflict more damage. "I figured marrying Harper would help me get over the fact that I couldn't have you."

Hands planted in her lap, she fidgeted, blinking up to the high-beamed ceiling before snapping her narrow-eyed gaze back down on me. "So you would have married someone else— someone you didn't love—without at least trying to tell me how you felt?"

"Asking Harper to marry me was the dumbest thing I've ever done."

"You didn't answer the question."

"What do you want from me, Macy?"

She got to her feet, then stomped over to the kitchen. "You didn't fight for me."

"Fight for you?" I scoffed, stalking after her, anger and confusion infused through my veins. "In my defense, I had no fucking clue you had feelings for me. You do realize you were active on dating apps, making it rain *'oh, he's just my best friend'* to every freaking guy you dated, right?"

She opened the fridge and before she could snag a bottle of water off the top shelf, I grabbed her elbow, spun her around, and slammed the door shut, pinning the blue-eyed beauty between me and the side-by-side stainless-steel monstrosity.

Breath hitching at my proximity, her eyes fluttered closed when I cupped the side of her face with one hand, planting my other hand on her delicate waist.

"Why would I have fought for a woman I didn't think I had a shot with? A woman who needs to own that she too could have opened her mouth and told me she was in love with me, instead of dating other guys, seemingly flaunting them in my face every chance she got."

She yanked my hand away from her face. "I didn't know how you felt about me and only dated them because I couldn't have you," she snapped, before her eyes widened as though realizing her own words proved my point. "Still, I never asked anybody to marry me."

"But it could have happened. You could have very well ended up with some guy you didn't love."

She shook her head and scoffed, mouth quivering as though angry it couldn't drip out a smart-mouthed retort.

"Look, baby." I snaked my arms around the small of her back. "We were both assholes for not fessing up, for not coming clean about how we felt. Truth is, if I hadn't proposed to Harper, the events that followed wouldn't have taken place. You wouldn't have gone out drinking with Sage and Chloe, and your digital diary never would have seen the light of day that kickstarted you and me, us, into place."

She pinned her gaze downward, and I commanded it right back up with the pad of my thumb raising her chin.

Searching her eyes, I said, "But, this has nothing at all to do with Harper or with me not fighting for you, does it?" I laid a soft kiss on her forehead. "You wanna tell me what's really going on, baby?"

She blinked, a tear trickling down her cheek. I swiped it away, only to watch another fall.

Fuck, I hated seeing her like that. Hated not being able to fix whatever was broken. "Don't cry, Macy," I whispered. "Just tell me what's wrong."

She swallowed, biting down on her lower lip as her eyes found mine. "I'm afraid when you get drafted, things are gonna change between us—and not in a good way. I've been sort of reading articles about couples who were together pre-draft, who inevitably break up post-draft." Her shoulders fell as she exhaled. "I'm scared that once you get out there, surrounded by fortune and fame, you'll get caught up in a moneyed lifestyle, parties, easy women, and destroy what we have, including our friendship." She sobbed. "I guess I'm scared you're gonna hurt me."

A knot of emotion clawed at my chest as my brain finally put two and two together. Macy had been acting slightly distant since my return from the Combine. Clueless me had chalked it up as her being overwhelmed with schoolwork, preparing for finals, graduation. Especially since I'd been a little overwhelmed myself, wondering if I'd be invited to attend Draft Day in person. The NFL only chose about thirty players each year to participate in the event live. I'd always been fixed on being chosen after Dad told me it was a once in a lifetime opportunity.

Draft Day was only a mere weeks away. No wonder she'd been a wad of emotion and affliction.

I pulled her into my arms, stroking her hair as she sobbed into my chest. "Never, baby. The only thing that's gonna change is how much more I plan to spoil you, shower you with everything you want."

She raised her head, our lips meeting in a sensual kiss that could have easily led to more. But since we were standing in her parents' kitchen, I wasn't able to scoop her up in my arms and carry her into our bedroom for the make-up fuck our heated bodies all but cried out for.

"I told you once before I'm yours forever, right?"

She nodded, a beautiful smile playing on her lips.

"Now, let's get home and spend the rest of the day and night having make-up sex we should have initiated about twenty-five seconds ago, *Macy Cake*."

~

NATIONAL FOOTBALL LEAGUE Official Draft Invite

Dear Lucas,

Congratulations on your outstanding college football career. Your accomplishments at UCLA have made you one of the highest-ranked players in this year's NFL Draft.

As a result, you and your family have the opportunity to join us at the draft on Thursday, April 25 at Nissan Stadium, Nashville. Many NFL players began their careers by being introduced live at the NFL draft.

The players who have been with us for the draft experience can tell you it was truly a "once-in-a-lifetime" opportunity, especially for their families. It is an important way for fans to get to know the top new players coming into our league, and we plan other activities to ensure that the trip is worthwhile and memorable.

Seth Moya, our Vice President of Football Communications, will contact you to discuss the arrangements. We are committed to doing everything possible to make your trip to Nashville a wonderful experience for you and your family. We hope you will join us.

Thank you for your consideration. I look forward to seeing you in Nashville.

Sincerely,

Tony Adwell, NFL Commissioner

28

MACY

NFL Draft Day Nashville, TENNESSEE

I felt like the girlfriend of a celebrity.

Red carpet events, meet and greets, paparazzi, not to mention a slew of microphone-wielding media, and that was just the first few hours.

We were treated like royalty, and I quickly realized how easy it was to get swept up in the life-of-a-star-athlete lifestyle.

"Oh, gosh. I need to pee again." Sage held her hand to the lower half of her belly, a scowl the size of the Mississippi River all over her face. "Help me find a bathroom, Macy."

We'd been enjoying events at the Draft Day Experience in downtown Nashville, hanging out while Lucas and AJ decided to step away from the party outside and hang out in their hotel room after taking photos and signing autographs. They were both anxious about the days ahead—Lucas a first-round pick and AJ a second-round pick.

It was Thursday, kick-off—pun highly intended—to the anticipated NFL Draft.

First-round picks always jumpstarted the events, and Lucas and his dad hoped he'd get snagged by one of the NFL's finest teams. I prayed for the best outcome, my heart soaring over the life-enhancing possibilities. Undeniably one of the best quarterbacks in college football history, it was a no-brainer that Lucas joined the pros and thrived. He deserved it, and I was honored to be one of those sitting by his side through it all. The spat that had me running like a crybaby to my parents' house ended up being the glue that made our relationship stronger, our love and respect for each other larger than life.

Downtown Nashville boomed, offering a free block-party-type event for all to hang out, listen to live music, eat, shop, and watch the draft live via one of the many jumbotrons. There were so many people in attendance, all trying to catch a glimpse of or receive an autograph from any or all of the prospective invited players, along with some big-name league players who stopped by.

"C'mon, there's a bathroom over by the Give Me Your Taco food truck."

"Ooh," she moaned, a ravenous tongue swiping her lips. "This baby's first word is going to be taco."

Turned out, Sage *was* pregnant and seemed to be quite taken by the idea of motherhood and marriage. AJ proposed at the doctor's office with a ring he'd apparently been holding onto since their high school graduation. Chloe filmed the entire thing, posting the video to UCChat right after. It was the cutest grand gesture ever, the whole doctor's office staff swooning.

"Can you grab me a taco while I go?" Sage batted her lashes, and of course, I caved. Besides, the smell of taco yumminess wafting in the air made my mouth water.

In line at the taco truck, I perused the schedule of the night's events on the Draft Day Experience app. Food, mini concerts, team merchandise booths, all booming before the big event, set to begin at 8 p.m. I'd planned on snagging merchandise from some of Lucas's favorite teams as souvenirs.

Two women around my age stood in front of me in line. They were gorgeous. Nice bodies. Perfect smiles. Brochures in hand, they were noticeably giddy over the list and photos of football players expected to attend the night's invite-only televised event.

The dark-haired one went nuts over some player I'd never heard of.

"Oh, my gosh!" she chirped. "Devon Smith is going to be here tonight. He's super-hot and well *equipped*," she tittered. "I hooked up with him at a postgame party when Utah played against us last fall."

I then noticed they were both wearing Arizona State sweatshirts, likely at Draft Day, supporting someone they knew, a friend or a relative perhaps.

The redhead continued looking over the attendees, her finger moving down the list, stopping suddenly. "Holy, shit! He's here. Lucas Hot Ass Stone."

My heart free-falled at the sound of *my* boyfriend's name oozing out of some other woman's mouth.

"You're so obsessed," said Dark-Haired Girl. "He's got a girlfriend, some nerdy book-obsessed blogger."

I'm not nerdy, is what I wanted to say, my insides churning like a cyclone.

"As long as he's not *married*," Red-Headed Slut said. "He's fair game."

I closed my eyes, basking in a cool and relaxing daydream of me grabbing a fistful of red hair and slamming her face into the ground. It was women like her—football groupie leeches—that made my skin crawl.

"Macy, are you falling asleep?" Sage's voice intruded my kick-the-bitch-in-her-ass fantasy.

I flicked my eyes open. "Nope, just thinking about how crazy my life is about to become." The thought made me just about lose my appetite for tacos.

Which didn't matter when Sage announced, "Um, the idea of shoving another taco in my mouth is gross." She pulled my arm, yanking me out of the line. "Let's get some froyo instead."

Time scrolled by, Sage and I dipping our toes in just about everything, and by the time 6 p.m. rolled around, we were beat.

Back in my hotel room, the anxiety streaming from Lucas was as potent as a contagious virus.

His agent, who'd been feverishly working behind the scenes, could be heard over speakerphone, spewing updates, while his dad kept feeding Lucas advice about said updates. Knowing nothing really about how the draft worked, I was lost. All I knew was that at eight, the first teams would pick from a list of eligible players—Lucas included—then announce their choice.

I could see the stress in my handsome jock's eyes even from where I stood, several feet away.

Walking over to him, our eyes locked, and I watched relief clean the look of anguish off of his face.

Gaze sparkling, he smiled and mouthed, "*I love you,*" pulling me into his arms.

Lips brushing against the shell of my ear, he said, "I can't wait until this whole thing is over so we can celebrate alone, just you and me," his voice low and swoony, slaying me with all the heart-to-toe-tingling feels.

Soon after, Lucas ended the phone call with his agent and his dad left to get dressed, saying he and his mom would meet us at the elevators at seven-thirty.

Lucas breathed out a noticeable sigh of relief as he plopped down onto the couch of the pretty swanky suite.

He patted his lap. "Come here, let's sit together for a minute, do a pulse check."

I climbed on top, straddling his lap as he ran his hands up and down my back, landing, then lingering on my butt. "How was your time with Sage? Any players out there try and take your fine ass back to their room?"

I giggled. "Only one, but I told him I was spoken for."

"That's my girl." He slapped my ass. "This is all mine."

I thought about my encounter with Red-Headed Slut. "You know, I did get a taste of what life may be like for me as the girl-friend of a hot pro football player." I ran my finger along the planes of his chest.

"Oh?" His eyebrows drew north. "Do tell."

I told him about the two women and what the trampy redhead said before I imagined bashing her face in. "I hate that my life could very well be like that. Every single day hearing other women talk about how hot my guy is."

Lucas shook his head, hands moving to the front of my shirt where his fingers began to unbutton my blouse. "Now you know how it feels."

I felt my eyebrows come together. "I'm sorry?"

He chuckled softly. "Baby, ever since high school—scratch that —ever since *middle* school, I've had to listen to friends, other foot-ball players, jerkholes, talk about how hot Macy Sinclair is. You have no idea how many fights I've gotten into over some asshat talking about what he wanted to do with you."

My face, neck, spine, even my toes, felt hot from embarrass-ment. I'd never been one to think guys, especially jocks, would refer to me as hot. "I-I had no idea."

He unfastened the last button on my shirt, biting his lower lip at the sight before him. "Well, when you have a hot best friend the struggle is undeniably real, even more so when that best friend becomes your girl. Point is, it doesn't matter what other people say or try to do. I'm not going anywhere, and I know neither are you. Don't let groupies bother you, just as I've stopped letting things horny guys say bother me."

With one hand busy on my butt, he drove the other through my hair, pulling slightly as his tongue swept across my neck.

"Enough of that shit." He nipped my lower lip, blue eyes full of fervor as I rocked against his growing bulge. "As usual, your sexy ass has made my cock hard. I think it's time we step into the shower."

29

LUCAS

E xuberance consumed me as I sat in the arena; the fans in the stands were already cheering, rallying out of control with excitement.

The anticipation of what would follow was like taking a shot of tequila and feeling the burn as it slid down my throat, on a slow and steady route to my gut. In other words, one must endure the bitter burn of the high before you get to enjoy it.

All the years I'd spent playing football, my dedication, my love, my knowledge of the game could've either be brought to an abrupt end or be elevated to a degree seen only in my dreams, in a matter of minutes.

Literally.

Each team in the first round had only ten minutes to make their pick—the shortest and longest ten minutes of my life.

Seated to my right were Mom and Dad, and to my left, Macy looking gorgeous in a dark blue body-hugging knee-length dress that complemented her figure and eyes. Beside her, sat Sage and AJ. As a second-round pick, he was expected to undergo the same level of stress the next day. After both receiving an exclusive invite to attend Draft Day events, the two of us agreed to partake in each other's sessions, giving our full brohood support.

NFL Commissioner, Tony Adwell, along with a few members of the hosting state's team, the Tennessee Titans, took to the podium, behind them, a sign that said "The Future Is Now."

The crowd exploded.

Hands intertwined, I brought Macy's to my mouth for a kiss, my leg bouncing erratically.

"Don't be nervous, handsome." She gave my hand a squeeze. "You *will* get picked. No doubt about it."

Tony's voice, the distinct timbre, sliced through the microphone, each syllable spoken sharp as a knife.

"Welcome, football fans, to this year's NFL Draft," he began. "Thank you all for being here to welcome our future NFL stars."

Mom leaned in and said, "I'm proud of you Son, so damn proud."

It meant a lot coming from her, having been against me playing football from the start after witnessing my father suffer through a career-ending knee injury.

Commissioner Adwell waited for the crowd to settle down before he announced the first team up for a pick. "Cleveland Browns are on the clock."

Always, the team that had the worst record last season picked first, and if I'm being honest, I was glad my name wasn't announced as that team's pick ten minutes later.

Tony announced the second team on the clock and again, I prayed they would not pick me. Sure, beggars can't be choosers, but as one of the nation's best college quarterbacks, I was hopeful.

However, when my name wasn't announced for pick three or pick four, panic began to settle in, especially when the team I wanted to play for, San Francisco, chose Sherlock Benson, who got booed by AJ and several others in the crowd as he walked on stage to shake the commissioner's hand. I spotted Harper in the crowd, cheering for her asshole of a man, which made me want to heave the way pregnant Sage did whenever she got a whiff of AJ's cologne.

"You okay?" Macy smiled up at me, our hands still intertwined.

I leaned over and kissed her forehead. "Just taking everything in."

When Tony announced the New York Jets were on the clock, hope bloomed in my chest. I'd never considered playing for an east coast team, my heart, and desires set on staying somewhere west.

The crowd buzzed as he returned back to the podium, those ten minutes that passed longer than summer solstice.

He cleared his throat as he opened the envelope. "The New York Jets pick Lucas Stone. Quarterback. UCLA."

My dad, Mom, AJ, everyone all cheered, patting me on the back, giving me hugs and high-fives.

I kissed Macy, then everything beyond that was a blur. I barely remember walking up on stage to shake Tony's hand and placing the Jets cap onto my head. But when I got back to my seat, I do remember my girl's face beaming, pride and excitement in her eyes.

Scooping her up, I kissed the sweet lips I never seemed to get enough of. "You ready to move to New York, baby?"

30

MACY

"The stars must be aligned for us."

With a grin wider than the sky, Chloe waved an eight-by-ten sheet of paper in the air as we all sat on the couch at their apartment. "This is my ticket to New York, too." She handed me the sheet of paper. "Well, at least for the summer, anyway."

It was an acceptance letter from *Hot Shot* magazine with details on the summer-intern program Chloe got accepted to.

"I guess since *Hot Shot's* winter internship filled up pretty quickly, they pushed some of the applicants to work during their summer internship program instead."

Sage snatched the paper from my hands. "Lucky girl. They haven't sent me anything."

I shrugged. "My name is probably at the top of their *do not hire* list."

"You guys?" Chloe stomped her foot like a two-year-old on the verge of a tantrum. "The whole point of the matter is, we'll all be in New York after graduation."

Her news was the icing on the cake to the whirlwind of events that had taken place in a matter of days following Draft Day.

The New York Jets picked AJ on day two of the draft, awarding him and Lucas their chance at being the next greatest quarterback and wide receiver duo.

Lucas had been talking nonstop with his agent who was feverishly trying to get him a sweet contract to sign. Everything about him becoming a pro baller was a strong brew of excitement and overwhelming sensations since it all had moved faster than lightning speed.

"You're right," I said, leaning over to hug Chloe. "You two have no idea how happy I am we will all be in the Big Apple together."

And I was happy.

About everything.

Living and working in New York was a journalist's dream. Almost every magazine I'd applied to was based there. To be able to live there with the guy of my dreams? Surreal.

"Let's order pizza to celebrate," Sage said, rubbing her belly that hadn't yet started showing signs she was pregnant. The only telltale sign was her having to pee every forty-five minutes and her never-ending appetite. "Maybe some chicken wings, too."

My phone vibrated with an incoming text from my baby.

Lucas: Hey, come home. We need to talk.

Catching me off guard, panic unfurled in my chest.

Me: Everything okay?

His reply came in immediately.

Lucas: Yep. Just come home, please.

Unease eating away at my belly, I told my besties goodbye, then headed out the door for my fifteen-minute drive home.

Once there, I found Lucas standing in the kitchen, back to the counter, looking trapped in some sort of daze. His eyes were a little red; the sight of him just standing there had curiosity clawing at my insides.

I padded over to him, reached up, and ran my fingers through his hair. "Baby? Everything okay?"

He grabbed my hand, brought it to his lips for a kiss. "My agent got back to me with the terms of the contract."

Inside my gut, excitement mingled with concern. "Okay? And..."

He pumped his chest as he coughed up the words. "Four years guaranteed. Thirty million. Twenty-million-dollar signing bonus."

Heartbeat shooting to the sky, I gasped. "Oh, my gosh. Lucas? Are you serious right now? Twenty. Million. Dollars?"

He chuckled almost as if in disbelief. "Baby, can you imagine what this means for us? Because this"—he picked up his phone from the counter, showing me the text from his agent before he set the phone back down—"doesn't even include endorsements from sponsors like Nike or whoever I decide to sign with."

I felt dizzy, heady, happy...and suddenly horny.

Evidently feeling the same, Lucas lifted me up and propped me on top of the counter.

He surveyed me with a smolder in his eyes that hit me right between the legs.

Bracketing my waist, he nudged my nose with his. "Marry me."

A smile tilted my lips. "Give me one reason why."

He pulled me close, settling between my thighs. "Baby, I can give you over thirty-million reasons why."

Arms draped around his neck, I bit down gently on his lower lip, something I'd learned drove him insane. "Money can't buy love, Mr. Stone."

With a moan, he unbuttoned his jeans, his cock visibly stiff through his designer boxer briefs.

"Oh, yeah? Tell me what can then?" His hands reached underneath my dress and found my thong, pulling the wet fabric to the side, finger massaging my throbbing clit.

"Orgasms," I breathed out, biting on my lower lip, watching as he worked out of his clothes, stroking his ready-for-me length. "Millions of orgasms."

He drove straight inside of me, my wet heat hugging his thick cock with greedy need.

His lips fanned against mine as he circled inside me, all the feels of that skilled pussy-pleasing maneuver already causing sensation to build. "Well, my sweet, sexy baby. I think I've just about got you covered."

ONLY MY SASSY mouth could ruin the makings of a sweet marriage proposal.

But after a night of love-fucking, Lucas brought it up again when he surprised me with breakfast he prepared while I was in the shower.

The smell of bacon drew me into the kitchen, the yummy scent wafting into the hallway.

"Have a seat, sleeping hottie." He was naked, save for a custom apron I got him for our Christmas gag gift exchange that said *MVP: Most Valuable Pussylicker* that he wore every time he prepared a meal.

Parking my T-shirt-only-wearing self onto one of the four chairs around the table, I watched my man prepare our plates, mouth watering over the sight of his perfectly tight, perfectly exposed ass.

"I'm not sure it's a good idea for you to be naked around me," I teased.

He spun around, two plates in one hand, coffees in the other, showing off his balancing act as he padded over to the table. "It's always a good idea for me to be naked around you." He waggled his brows.

Lowering the items onto the table, he eased onto the chair

beside me, leaning in for a kiss. "Good morning, baby. Thought you might be a little hungry after we skipped dinner last night."

I was hungry, starving in fact, and wasted no time digging into the plate of scrambled eggs, bacon, toast, and sliced strawberries —the Lucas Stone breakfast specialty.

We chatted more about his contract, salary, and signing bonus, the totality of it all still not quite sinking in.

Taking a bite of bacon, my eyes caught the glimmer of something silver under the cloud of scrambled eggs. With my fork, I moved the eggs around on the plate, my heart freezing when I realized the silver, glittery thing was a ring.

A ring!

With a gasp, my hands went over my mouth, heart galloping around my chest chanting, *Oh, my God. Oh my God. Oh, my God.*

Lucas removed the ring from the plate, holding the eye-catching gem between his index finger and thumb as he got down on one knee, scooting my chair around so I could face him.

"Baby..." He peered up at me, intoxicated gaze swimming with mine. "No one else will ever hold my heart, love me, the way you do, and I promise no one will hold your heart, adore, appreciate, and protect you the way I do." He paused for a moment and breathed. "Seems from day one we've been a love story in the making, and this ring will guide us toward our happily-forever-after." He took hold of my left hand, kissing it tenderly. "Let's hold our hearts in each other's hands for life. Marry me, baby."

My hand quivered in his—actually, my whole body shook— and it was useless to try and stop the stream of tears racing down my face.

That proposal melted me, claiming my heart, body, and soul from the first few words.

And after I all but screamed, "Yes," he slid the five-carat-diamond beauty onto my finger with ease before scooping me up in his Thor-like arms, carrying me into our bedroom and onto the bed.

For the next thirty minutes, no words were exchanged while he devoured, kissed, and licked every inch of my body, the two of us coming together in a soiree of love, lust, and insatiable desire. We lay in bed afterward, falling asleep in each other's arms, basking in thoughts of our future, thoughts of what was meant to come.

31

MACY

Weeks fly by when you're prancing around on cloud nine.

And with graduation quickly approaching, along with the list of events that would bring Lucas closer to the start of his NFL career, I was surprised I still knew how to breathe.

Life for us got a little cray-cray after Lucas proposed. I went on a few interviews for some of the magazines I'd applied to—some in person and some via Skype, uncertain if I'd made a lasting impression. Then, a week later, Lucas took me with him to New York to sign his pretty spectacular contract, the money from his signing bonus hitting his account hours later.

Looking at all those zeros, floored me—him, too. But before Lucas scheduled time to meet with his accountant back in Los Angeles, he wanted to take advantage of our weekend in New York. Dinner, a Broadway show. Horse and carriage ride through Central Park. A selfie in front of the famous Sex and the City Brownstone that Sage, Chloe, and I never got a chance to go to, even though it was on our Single In New York things-to-do list.

Lucas surveyed the brownstone's picturesque facade. "We need to buy a house."

"We? Don't you mean, *you*?" Who knew why my mouth said stupid shit sometimes, exposing my mile-long list of insecurities.

"It's *our* money, baby, *our* life. Don't get weird about it, okay?" He pulled me into his arms. "Now tell me, Penthouse in Manhattan or Brownstone in Soho?"

We spent the next day touring properties with a real estate agent recommended by his agent, square feet upon luxury square feet wooing my eyes and heart. I'd always dreamed of a life in New York, albeit a less fancy one, complete with roommates and a pet ferret, like Jen A's character in the movie *Along Came Polly*. I was overwhelmed, dazed, and even crazier in love with a guy who was offering me the world.

After viewing over a dozen highly-priced potential abodes, Lucas and I asked to see one of the lesser-priced ones—an enormous six thousand square-foot, six-bedroom penthouse condo, complete with a doorman, located in the heart of Tribeca. We immediately fell head over heels for everything, the condo's modern decadence swallowing our hearts.

Lucas linked his hand with mine as we walked through the gourmet kitchen. "This feels like us, doesn't it, baby?" He made sure the real estate agent was out of earshot. "I can see myself fucking you from behind right up against that cool marble counter."

I hushed him, my face feeling flush, clit fanning herself. "You better behave yourself before the pearl-clenching real estate agent runs out of here after getting a glimpse of that anaconda-sized bulge in your pants."

We ended up making a cash offer on the Tribeca condo, the agent assuring Lucas the offer would be accepted right away. Sure enough it was, the text notification striking Lucas's phone as we were boarding our flight back to Los Angeles.

〜

"Looks like everything's falling into place for you two." Mom sipped on cinnamon-stick coffee as I sat beside her on the swing in my parents' enormous backyard.

I inhaled the hot brew in my cup, cinnamon tickling my nose before I sipped. "Yep, sure is."

Mom rocked the swing back and forth, a pair of vetting eyes assessing me. "What's the matter?"

I shook my head in denial. "Nothing. Everything is great."

"Macy Cake?" she probed.

Hesitantly, I opened up. "It's just that I feel like..." I trailed off, not wanting to say what had plagued my mind because, in all honesty, life was shaping up pretty damn spectacularly. New home to go to when we finally moved to New York after gradua-tion; access to the clothing from sponsors Lucas signed with; the promise of a lifestyle envied by most women all over the world; a fairy-tale wedding on my birthday in front of family and friends in October.

Mom's finger grazed the bottom of my chin, tilting my head up and over to meet her gaze. "Honey, you can tell me anything."

Fighting hesitance, I spoke softly, as if the low tone would be a veil that would mask my words. "Lucas has promised me the world, and I love him for that, love that he has no expectations of me contributing financially. But I want success too, *my own* success, a career in journalism, a career in writing."

"Honey, you are moving to New York City, a place full of reputable magazines that you can apply to. I'm sure one of them will—"

"I've already received an offer," I interjected. "From *Cosmo*."

"Wow, sweetie," she squealed. "That's awesome! I know you've always dreamed of working for them. When did you get the offer? And what's the position?"

"Got the phone call from the HR director yesterday, followed by an email with the official offer. It's super entry-level, assistant to a social media director, no doubt doing very assistant-cliché duties like coffee runs, etcetera. They're giving me up till four weeks after graduation to accept or turn it down." I stared straight ahead at the swimming pool, my voice now monotone. It was the first time I'd shared the news aloud; sharing the news via text with Chloe and Sage seemed easier, and I made them both promise to die before they told Lucas.

"Okay? We all know magazine jobs start at the bottom."

I nodded, aware that I'd always have to start low, never expecting to get lucky enough to receive the same grand-slam offer like the one I dissed from *Hot Shot*.

"So, what's the problem, sweetie?" Mom reached over and tucked a loose strand of hair behind my ear.

Unease whirled wildly in my belly, a glacier-sized chunk of anguish lodged in my throat. "The position is based in London, England."

32

LUCAS

ookie Minicamp.

A three-day mixture of meet and greets, studying the team playbook, then putting plays into action on the field. Sadly some players—signed contract or not—don't make it past minicamp, and I wanted to be sure my name didn't end up on the list of those asked to pack up and call it 'never happening'.

"Sage and I bought a house in Jersey," AJ breathed out, setting the weights back onto the bar. "I'll pick up the keys before we head back to Los Angeles."

We were working out, taking turns spotting each other at the bench press.

"I thought you planned to buy something in New York like Macy and I did?" I said, remembering our conversation a few weeks back clearly. I mean he received a pretty decent signing bonus and contract, as well.

AJ lifted the weights, brought it to his chest, and breathed out. "Well, with the baby on the way, we wanted to be sure I'm only a few miles away, instead of several miles and traffic jams away from home. Besides"—he pushed the weights off his chest and slammed them back onto the bar—"we found a pretty dope three-acre home with a pool that Sage just about died over."

I thought about moving to New Jersey, as well, since the Jets home stadium was actually in Jersey instead of New York, contrary to what some may think.

But I knew how much Macy loved New York, and I would have done anything necessary to keep her happy, see that all of her dreams come true, too.

"Well, we'll still be in the same time zone, so don't be surprised when Macy and I drive over to your house on weekends to pay a visit to you two and the kiddo whenever it finally arrives."

"October," he said, sitting up, wiping beads of sweat off his face and neck. "The baby is due in October."

"That's the month we plan to get married—Macy's birthday, October thirteenth."

AJ told me that the baby was due October fifth, assuring me they'd make it to our wedding.

"You better make it to the wedding." I chuckled. "Considering you're the best man."

It was still hard to believe he was going to be a dad, and that he and Sage were going to get married. At the same time, I never imagined I'd be marrying Macy, never imagined moving to New York, never imagined playing for the Jets.

33

MACY

"Girl, that dress makes you look sick." Sage lounged on the leather sofa between Mom and Chloe, sparkling apple juice in one hand, cucumber and smoked-salmon tea sandwich in the other. "And by sick, I mean *hot*."

Chloe glared at her, then scoffed, tossing her tea sandwich back onto her plate, clearly more annoyed than she needed to be. "Then just tell her the dress makes her look *hot*. Sick actually means sick again. Sick-Hot is so five years ago."

Sage rolled her eyes. "Oh, you mean like your bangs?"

"No," Chloe seethed. "More like that prune-colored lipstick you wear every day like it's your job."

"Ugh!" I stomped my foot. "You two have been fighting nonstop yesterday and today. This is supposed to be *my* day to shop for a wedding dress, not supervise a pair of teenaged women."

We were at Bliss Wedding Boutique as I shopped for my wedding dress—a day typically meant for fun times instead of the bitchy whining-times vibe Sage and Chloe had sprinkled it with.

Mom sighed. "She's right, ladies. Cut Macy some slack, huh?

At least until she walks out on that pedestal and we all gasp and gawk because she's finally found the perfect gown."

I blew Mom a kiss, then marched back to the dressing room to slip into dress number seven.

Exhausting. Irritating.

That's what my few days with my besties had felt like—despite the fact I'd planned a big three-day time-with-my-girls fest. Or maybe I'd just been riding the cranky train since Lucas had been away at Rookie Minicamp for two days. I was straight out addicted to that man and couldn't seem to breathe without him.

I shimmied out of the mermaid-style dress, soft fabric falling around my ankles. Ginger, the boutique's dressing assistant, scooped it up after I stepped out of the silk puddle and hung it back onto its hanger.

"Is it always this hard to find *the* dress, or am I just one of the unlucky ones?" I asked, beginning to feel hopeless. After perusing their catalog, I'd thought it would take minutes, not hours to come across a dress that would make everyone melt.

Ginger shook her head. "Mmm-mmm. Last week, Katie Turner, that gorgeous YouTube makeup tutorial sensation, took twelve hours." She blinked. "Twelve. Before she finally settled on a cute little diamond-studded minidress. Wanna know the secret in finding the perfect dress?" She helped me get into dress number seven, zipping the back closed before spinning me around to face the mirror. "Just. Breathe."

My breath hitched, fingers hovering over my open mouth.

The dress was heart-stopping with a draped bodice on this sort of flounced-looking tulle ballgown, layered over more sequined tulle, with a crystal beaded waistband.

Ginger wept, either tears of joy because she knew I'd finally found the gown, or tears of joy because she thought I looked as beautiful as I felt.

"It's perfect," she said. "You look like a bride now."

Stepping onto the pedestal, the dress's exquisite jewels glittering under the lights, Sage, Chloe, and Mom let out a collective hand-over-heart gasp.

"Mom?" My weepy eyes flicked over to her for a verbal approval, but all she could do was nod over and over again, tears streaming down her face.

"Chloe?" I looked at my best friend.

"I'm actually speechless right now." She fanned her face, doing her best to keep tears at bay.

I glanced over to my other best friend, whose eyes were surveying me, up and down. "Sage? What do you think?"

Sage nodded. "I'd totally marry you."

THAT NIGHT, I crawled into bed, scooting over to the side Lucas always slept on. I inhaled the scent of his cologne on the pillow—I'd unashamedly sprayed some of the fragrance there the first night he left for minicamp.

God, I was such a lunatic.

Or maybe it was normal to feel empty inside when the man you were crazy in love with was away from home.

Which got me thinking of *Cosmo's* job offer in London. If I accepted the position—which I hadn't yet—lovestruck me would likely die of Lucas Stone starvation, considering he was the only thing feeding my soul.

Thankfully, I still had time to think it over, ponder all the pros and cons, purposely holding back from mentioning anything about it to Lucas, allowing him time to bask in his own glory while I thought it over. True, having wanted to work for *Cosmo* since practically forever, it was a dream opportunity, regardless of how low I'd have to start.

But, Lucas was also my dream, my heart's wish come true.

Sitting in bed, laptop open as I typed, I then posted my *Confessions of a Bookaholic* review for Alessandra Torre's latest release, when my phone vibrated. A text from my Lucas Stone.

Lucas: You awake?

A smile warmed my face.

Me: Just got into bed. Isn't it late there?

Lucas: Yep. Close to midnight. Went out with AJ and some of the other guys on the team to celebrate making it through camp.

Me: You deserve it, baby. Congrats.

Text bubbles bounced on the screen, then they disappeared, leaving me with nothing in return. I lay there pouting. Like a goddamn baby.

Seconds later, I jumped, startled when my phone rang, Lucas's name and face flashing on the screen, beckoning for a FaceTime call.

I patted my freshly showered locks into place, then activated the chat, his sultry smirk lighting up my heart.

"Hey," he said in that cool-hot Lucas Stone tone. He was in bed, propped up against the headboard, shirtless.

"Hey." I beamed back. "No fair showing me a naked chest I can't lick and claw at over the phone."

"Show me yours."

I tried not to giggle, but, of course, failed miserably. "Don't you dare *'girls gone wild'* me, Mr. Stone and ask me to lift my shirt on video."

"I miss you, baby, miss hearing you giggle in person, having you curled up beside me, watching your eyes flutter closed as you fall asleep."

"I miss you, too, even sprayed cologne all over your pillowcase."

He chuckled. "That's cute. How was wedding dress shopping? I saw your 'found it' post on UCChat."

I explained how fabulous my dress looked, plus all the ways Chloe and Sage got on my last nerves.

"AJ showed me a picture of their house in Jersey, mentioned they're not getting married until December." He yawned, resting his head atop a fluffy pillow. "And how their baby is due in October."

"Right." I sighed. "Two weeks before our wedding. And just our luck, she'll go into labor the day before, leaving us without a best man or a maid of honor."

"Won't matter because nothing could ruin our wedding. I'd marry you even if it was just the two of us, if you'd let me. But I know you've had your heart set on a big wedding on your birthday and you deserve to always have what you want."

God, he was perfectly, perfect.

"Hurry up and get back home to me so I can sit on your handsome face," I insisted.

"Yep, catching the 6 a.m. flight, so I should be home tomorrow a little after noon. You better be waiting for me, naked in bed." He blew me a kiss. "Love you forever, baby."

"Forever and ever."

34

MACY

June fourteenth.

A day I'd been striving for since I walked onto UCLA's campus four years before.

Graduation.

One of life's greatest achievements, not only for me as the student, but for my parents too.

As soon as my eyes sprang open that morning, excitement came over my skin in waves.

"You did it, Macy Cake." Mom's face glowed with pride. "All these years of studying, working toward your degree and, look at you," she said, eyes gleaming as she rubbed my shoulders, "graduating with honors."

Dad pulled us into a Sinclair-family group hug, my heart dancing. Truth is, that public display of affection used to embarrass me when I was too young to know better. "Congrats, sweetheart. You've made your old folks proud."

I found my seat in a row where Sage, Chloe, AJ, and Lucas were seated, the five of us with bittersweet feelings about our last day together on campus.

"We did it, guys," Chloe yelped. "Once we walk across that

stage, we'll have no choice but to put our adult underpants on and suck the shit out of life."

"I'm proud of us all," Sage declared, chin up. "Beyond happy we've stuck it out, endured four years of this shit without saying 'fuck it' like I wanted to do at least eighty-seven thousand times."

Relief gripped my chest, grateful it all was nearing an end; like Sage, I too had moments when I wanted to throw in the towel and hide in the bushes.

AJ and Lucas were busy chatting about football stuff, graduation to them now seemingly an insignificant stepping pebble to our pretty significant stepping stone toward our careers—although ever since Sage had realized she was pregnant, she stopped showing any interest in chasing her career dreams.

Maybe that's what I needed—a baby to quell my off-and-on itch to chase my career aspirations.

THREE DAYS AFTER, Lucas and I prepared for our official move to New York.

We alternated between spending a day with my parents, then his, where emotional farewells were equally high.

"I've always known you were meant for him," Lucas's mom said, handing me a glass of iced tea.

His dad chimed in. "Yep. When he kicked that clown at your birthday party, I imagined an older Lucas and Macy walking down the aisle."

All of us took part in a lengthy laugh at the memory, Lucas's face a bright cherry red.

We sat around the pool, enjoying the sun, antipasto salad, and cake decorated with New York Jets colors and the number seven, Lucas's jersey number.

"Lucky number seven." Lucas winked at me with a squeeze to my thigh.

I knew my face turned red, remembering his reference to me being his lucky number seven that night he went down on me for the first time.

LATER, when I was helping his mom clear the dishes from dinner, she shared feedback about life with a pro football player.

"Can I offer you some advice?" She passed a glass over to me and I placed it on the top rack of the dishwasher.

"Always."

"Let Lucas spoil you, give you the world. He'll be working hard out on that field, taking blow after blow, and the highlight for him —besides winning—will be the satisfaction, the relief and pride of knowing his woman is well taken care of, happy as all heck, waiting for him at the end of every game."

I blinked away tears, guilt stabbing me in each eye. The fact she didn't pursue her career until after Lucas's dad retired, bloomed like a corpse flower in my face. "Is that why you didn't open your psychology practice until he retired?"

She bobbed her head. "God knows I wanted to before then, but I needed to be at every game, needed to be there cheering him on, supporting my man, especially in the event he got injured. Being his rock became my career and I did it like a boss, a badass baller's wife for ten years."

Ice coated my heart, visions of Lucas collapsing onto the green, recalling the sinking feeling of helplessness I felt three thousand miles away, unable to get to him for hours. The pain that coursed through my body then was something I never wanted to relive again.

When Lucas and I were ready to leave that night, I hugged her tightly, thanking her for such sound advice—a peek under the tent of football life.

Little did she know, her advice helped me decide what to do about *Cosmo's* offer waiting for me in London.

"WELL, THIS IS IT, BABY." Lucas squeezed my waist as we stood in the living room of the empty space we'd called home for the last four years. "Lots of memories here. Parties, late nights spent on the couch studying, our first full-blown roommate argument over toothpaste..."

I cracked up at the memory. "You were wrong for not putting the cap back on the toothpaste, plain and simple."

His eyebrows piqued. "I've never left the cap off since." He pulled me close to him. "We've also had some pretty unforgettable firsts here. Our first kiss," he whispered as he brushed his lips against mine, "plus the first time I got to taste you."

Our lips and tongues met with fury, heat, and greed as we feverishly worked each other out of our clothes.

"One more memorable fuck for the road paved forward," Lucas rasped, our naked bodies crashing onto the cool linoleum where we bid a proper goodbye to our old life, ready to grasp onto the new one awaiting us three thousand miles away.

35

LUCAS

"**L**et's stay here."

My inebriated perusal cruised over Macy, drunk over the off-white dress that hugged her beautiful body, pausing on the mouthwatering contours of her breasts—an outline of her pebbled nipples visible through the fabric—then lingering on delicious hourglass curves.

"We need to go," she reasoned, her voice laced with laughter as she took five steps backward in an effort to keep my grabby hands at bay. "It's your first team party." She backed into a wall by the door of our Tribeca condo. "We need to go even if it's only for a few hours."

Hands planted in my trouser pockets, I trekked over to her slowly, allowing my hungry eyes more time to drink her in. "Fine, we'll go. But keep in mind," I warned as I stood in front of her, fingering a lock of golden-blond hair, taking in the ragged rise and fall of her chest. "I'm fucking you during our limo ride home."

The New York Jets Official Welcome Ball.

A formal meet and greet with players, coaches, staff, cheer-leaders, you name it.

Held at the luxurious Bogota Hotel in New Jersey, it was an

annual pre-training camp soiree complete with a live band, dancing, food, and plenty of liquor.

As we stepped out of the limo, members of the paparazzi called out my name, snapping our photos as I guided Macy to the entrance.

Her dress was backless, the opening kissing the small of her back, and when my hand slid over her hip, I didn't feel a panty line.

I leaned in as we walked around the ballroom in search of our assigned table and whispered, "Are you wearing *nothing* under this dress?"

Her lips fanned my ear. "I wouldn't call my birthday suit *nothing*, Mr. Stone."

Speech. Less.

Seated at our assigned round table we found AJ and Sage, along with another wide receiver, Damian Hicks, a known playboy from Arizona State.

We exchanged pleasantries, introducing one another to our significant others.

Sage, whose belly had begun to show she was indeed expecting, gawked at Macy. "Girl, you look gorgeous. That dress looks painted on you."

Macy smiled as I pulled out her chair, her cheeks turning pink to match the table's floral centerpiece.

Music blared and servers were making their rounds, some with trays of wine, champagne, and bottled water, others with appetizers.

"You both had a tight record at UCLA," Damian said to me and AJ. "We used to study your plays, your team's formations. Glad to be on the same team with you guys this time around."

The Ball was okay. Good food. Music. A great time to mingle and meet veteran players and rookies.

But I couldn't keep my gaze off of Macy.

Besides her long, blond hair and angelic smile, it was that dress she wore, showcasing her slender yet curvaceous body that had my eyes on lockdown, my cock jumping and panting.

Knowing she was completely nude under the dress, getting a subtle reminder each time the knee-high split at the front exposed her legs, well, I was fucked...or at least I desperately wanted to be fucked.

And while on the dance floor, holding her body close, I leaned in and murmured, "You're about to get fucked in the limo."

Her hand in mine, we made our way out to the waiting car, shaking hands, saying goodbyes along the way.

And when we made it outside to the limo, I told the driver, "Crank up the music on the drive home, please."

"Anything particular, Mr. Stone?" the driver asked.

"Drake."

I eased into the limo, eyes on Macy, who sat with her legs crossed as if she were trying to shield her pussy from the damage I was about to inflict.

Music cranked high, I activated a switch that raised the privacy screen as our limo sped off.

I slid to the middle of the seat, grabbing a gentle hold of Macy's wrist. "Come here, baby." I licked my lips. "I want you over here. Right on my lap."

She settled on top, legs straddling me as I ran my hands up and down her back. I wanted to touch all of her at once, fighting the urge to bend her over, lift up that dress, and fuck her hard and fast.

My cock swelled, practically unzipping my fly all on its own, as she rolled her hips around me, mouth open, welcoming my tongue.

Fingers tangled in her hair, I hissed, "You can't do this to me, baby."

"Do what?" she teased, brandishing that spicy smirk, fully aware her snark held a one-way ticket to Fuck Me Ville.

Tugging the hem of her dress, I dragged the smooth fabric up and over her hips, exposing her bare ass, bare sex. "You can't wear this"—I plucked the dress over her head, my eyes fucking her luscious curves, and whispered—"with nothing but your ridiculously hot body underneath."

Lamplights from the highway gleamed through the windows, casting a soft glow inside the limo, her bombshell body shimmering in the night. I could've sat there and stared at her forever, always mesmerized by her beauty.

I sucked her right nipple in my mouth, circling the left with my thumb, her back arching as her fingers pulled on my hair. "*Oh, Lucas.*"

Fuck, the sultry hum that escaped from her lips was like a direct message to my cock.

I'd waited all night to be deep inside her—fuck that—I'd waited since the second I saw her in that dress, and our night of foreplay was over and done.

"Raise up, baby, and turn around," I told her, freeing my cock from my pants.

Back facing me, she straddled my lap and I guided her hips down, easing her pussy onto my eager cock.

She rocked up and down, her hands pushing on my thighs for support.

"*Fuck*, Macy," I moaned, as she leaned into me, my palms cupping her breasts, fingers pulling her nipples. "You're so hot, so wet, always so...fucking...tight."

The rock and roll of her hips met my thrusts head-on, the *boom-boom* of the music masking the sounds of her wet body slapping against mine.

"Oh, *God,* Lucas," she breathed out. "Please, I need *more.*"

My finger found her clit, massaging it, rubbing it as she rode my cock harder, faster.

"Come, baby," I said, my voice demanding and gruff, her so-good pussy morphing me into a sex-crazed alpha every single time. "You know I need you to come."

Her pussy gripped my cock, squeezing it as she quaked against me, the pulsing sensation taking me right there with her, the orgasm streaming through me like a bolt of lightning.

Christ, how we must have looked in that limo, my pants and boxers pooled around my ankles, her straddling me in nothing but high heels, the two of us panting, bodies glistening with sex.

I helped her off me and she moved around to face me, gaze still swimming with lust.

She kissed me, tender, sweet as her palms cupped my face. "I'm proud to be yours, Lucas Stone, honored to be your future wife." Her eyes were misty with tears that I wasn't sure if I'd caused to fall. "No matter what, I'll always be by your side, cheering you on."

I held her tight, planting light kisses on her forehead. "Me too, baby. Me too."

SOMETIMES, when parents give you advice, it doesn't sink in, until you're living the moment.

If she has career dreams, encourage her to pursue them. Your mom put her career dreams on hold while I was out there on the gridiron living mine. Sure, she seemed happy standing by my side, but I've always wondered if she would have been even happier doing what her heart desired sooner rather than later.

It's what Dad told me the night before Macy and I left for New York—his heart-to-heart advice to me while Macy and Mom were busy cleaning the kitchen.

Little did I know, his advice would sound in my head like an ambulance two weeks later.

It was two days after the Welcome Ball. I'd gone to AJ's house to pick him up for a workout regimen we'd agreed to do with a bunch of other rookie players. With training camp only a week away, we all wanted to condition our bodies for what was to come.

"You ready to go, Bro?" I stood in the foyer of AJ's house at 9 a.m. as planned.

"Yeah..." He scratched his head. "But Sage is bitching about me not leaving until I eat the breakfast she made."

I chuckled. "You're a pussy."

Inside his kitchen, Sage greeted me with a smile. "Hey, next time bring Macy so we can hang out while you two monsters work out."

I parked myself onto the stool at their breakfast bar, admiring the farm-style decor. Their home was pretty cool, something to raise a kid or two in, something that had future written all over the seven thousand or so square feet of space.

AJ sat next to me, digging into the plate of food Sage prepared for him, licking his fingers like a savage.

"I'll bring her next time," I told Sage. "Today she was too busy applying for an internship with a few, local, small-scaled magazines."

Sage slid a plate of food over to me. "So, Macy's decided not to accept *Cosmo's* offer?" She shook her head, not bothering to wait for my reply. "That sucks considering she lost out on that badass opportunity to work for *Hot Shot,* too."

"Wait. What do you mean?" I pushed the plate over, curious about what Sage was babbling on about.

"Remember last year when we all came to New York for that week-long interview?"

I nodded.

"Well, Macy was offered a full-time job. I don't recall the

details, but it had something to do with her blog. Only she wasn't able to fulfill the last part of her interview assignment because she took off back to Los Angeles when you collapsed on the field with that concussion."

Pain raked my chest as I forced myself to remember what Macy said when I'd asked her if she'd been able to complete that last assignment during the interview—albeit she failed to mention the job offer altogether.

Yep, was all she said, before changing the subject.

Fuck.

"And what about this *Cosmo* offer?"

AJ coughed. "Dude, she hasn't told you anything?"

I shook my head. "If she did, I wouldn't be sitting here with my ass in my hand, looking to you two for answers."

"Then Sage probably shouldn't tell you either." He gave his woman a look and I wanted to punch him.

"Bro, believe me, she can tell me now that the seed has been planted."

Sage bit down on her lip, guilt carving a line between her eyebrows. "She's going to kill me."

I shot up from the stool, hating that I had to stand there, ready to beg for information that probably should have come from my woman's mouth in the first place. "I won't tell her you told me."

Sage looked to her man for approval, and he gave her a nod.

"Well, Macy had interviewed with a few big-named magazines, still hoping one would offer her something in New York."

Jaw ticking, I leaned against the stool, urging her to go on.

"Apparently, *Cosmopolitan* got back to her weeks before graduation, offering her an entry-level position as an assistant to their social media director. I think she only has about two weeks left to accept or decline their offer."

It was awesome news, especially since *Cosmopolitan* had an office in Manhattan.

Sage rubbed her growing belly. "As you can imagine, it's a dream job for someone who's lived for a career in journalism. I know for a fact, Macy was heartbroken over the *Hot Shot* mishap, and *Cosmo's* offer was the glue to mend it."

Arms folded over my chest, I shrugged, unsure of why she seemed to be hesitating. "Okay, so she accepts the offer and starts working for *Cosmo*. What's the big deal?"

Sage cleared her throat and quietly said, "Lucas, the job is in London."

Thanks to high school Geography, I knew there were three US cities named London. "Okay, so London Ohio, Arkansas, or Kentucky?" Hope bloomed wide in my chest, because if it were any of those three cities, fuck it, we could make the distance between us work.

Sage shook her head, gaze flicking to her man, then right back to me. "London, England."

Grabbing my keys, I trekked toward the front door. Head on fire. Mission: Unknown.

AJ called after me. "Hey, what about our workout?"

"Not today, dude," I grumbled over my shoulder. "I've got shit to figure out."

36

T hey say the honeymoon phase doesn't last forever.

Ours lasted so long, I thought for sure we were the power couple to prove that ill-fated theory wrong. We were sailing along on our little love boat, free of choppy waves, hurricanes, and catastrophic icebergs.

Until we weren't.

About one week before Lucas had to report for training camp, something seemed to change.

He barreled in the house, drunk out of his mind one night.

"Lucas, are you *drunk*?"

He swayed on his feet. "Didn't know I was shacking up with Captain Obvious."

He became short with me, making it rain one- or two-worded replies aplenty...

"Want to go out for pizza, tonight?"

"No."

"Hey, are you excited about your first pro training camp?"

"Yep."

"Wanna join me in the shower?"

"Not today."

"Lucas, is everything all right?"

"Everything's great."

Then he began to distance himself, attending longer than normal workout sessions, hanging out in Jersey hotspots for drinks with guys from the team—never once inviting me.

I swear he did small stuff—like leave the cap off the toothpaste —to irritate me.

"You left the cap off the toothpaste this morning."

"Oh."

Whenever I initiated sex, he came up with excuses like needing to preserve his energy for the gym.

My plethora of insecurities lunged at me gripping a pitchfork laced with a lethal dose of self-doubt.

It's the five pounds of weight I gained.

He's had enough of spending too much time with me.

It's only toothpaste.

Who needs sex every night anyway?

He's lying.

On the morning he left for training camp, I got nothing but a peck on the cheek and a, "See ya," before he took off with Damian Hicks who was, of course, behind the wheel of a flashy McLaren convertible.

What the fuck?

Head ready to explode, my thumbs went ballistic, pounding the keys of my phone, blasting off a text to give him a big piece of my mind.

Me: Look, you asshole. I'm not going to see your grumpy ass for three weeks—save for the weekends you get to come home for a visit—and all I get is a measly, kiss-your-sister kind of peck on the cheek and a shitty, motherfucking "see ya"?

Phone in my shaky hand, I glared at the text, bare feet hitting the cool tile, pacing our kitchen floor as my chest inhaled a combination of sobs and ragged breaths.

Press. Send.

You know the jerkbag deserves it.

But I couldn't send it. Couldn't send him off to training camp as angry—*hurt*—as I was.

Instead, I dispatched words straight from the eyes of reason rather than the angry haze blurring the lines between my fuming head and my bleeding heart.

Me: Miss you already! Hope we can talk about whatever is bothering you when you come home for training camp break this weekend.

He never replied.

∿

THE THREE DAYS that followed had me feeling as though I'd been hit by an asteroid.

I barely heard from Lucas, and when I did, his replies were blunt and dry.

Me: You think we can FaceTime tonight?

Lucas: Maybe.

Adding salt to my wounds, were the social media posts of Lucas that showed him seemingly partying with Damian Hicks. Seeing the two of them surrounded by tall libations and beautiful women, picked at my unhealed scab of fears of him partying, tossing money around, meeting another woman, and hurting me.

Thoughts swirled in my head, questioning whether or not *this* was going to be the story of my life. Synopsis: *What Happens When A Book Blogger Accidentally Publishes Her Digital Diary Online? A Viral Shitstorm.* The first few chapters—even the middle—are unforgettable, the last chapters, however, filled with pages that lead to a bitter disappointment of no happily-ever-after.

Loneliness whacked me like an axe. Everyone I knew out of reach.

Sage decided to spend the month with her parents all the way in Buttcrack, Nebraska. And Chloe was slammed, interning at *Hot Shot,* hating and loving the rush that had her too beat for words with no desire to hang out with pitiful me.

I could have reached out to Mom, cried on her virtual shoulder, but I didn't want to hint a witch's brew of darkness was around me, my pride too thick to penetrate.

Lucky for me, our condo happened to be in one of New York's trendiest of cities. Tribeca was life, vibrant decadence that my crushed soul craved. And when I ventured out on my own, I ended up getting my food to go, too annoyed, saddened by happy couples practically shoving their public displays of affection down my throat.

I was gone, dead inside, unable to grasp how my rock met bottom so fast.

Saturday came, and I was looking forward to my Lucas being home that weekend, a time for us to talk, clear the air, resurrect a love, an unbreakable bond that, for reasons unknown, was on a flight destined to crash and burn.

But an hour before he was expected home, I was met with a text message that may as well have been a firebomb to my heart.

Lucas: Not gonna make it home this weekend.

37

LUCAS

Strategy.

It's how the game is played.

Plans of action or plays used to move the ball down the field, closer to the goal.

I needed to move Macy down the field, so to speak. Move her closer to achieving her dream, closer to her goal.

MACY: Why aren't you gonna make it home this weekend?

GOD, I could almost hear, *feel*, her heart crumbling as she typed that text, because, truth is, mine did, too.

Dread filled my stomach, the agony of hurting her ripping every fiber of my being.

I hated being the dick who didn't answer her calls or reply to texts, hated being the asshole who went out drinking with teammates, surrounding myself with other women, hated being the fuckwad who didn't come home.

I knew that hurt her, a blow below the belt she didn't deserve.

Fuck, it hurt—*destroyed*—me to emotionally torture the woman I so desperately loved.

But at the time, it was the best strategy, the best way to get Macy to accept *Cosmo's* job offer in London. If she didn't, odds were she would have ended up hating me down the line anyway. See, after Sage spilled all the tea, Dad's advice popped to mind.

Your mom put her career dreams on hold while I was out there on the gridiron living mine... I've always wondered if she would have been even happier doing what her heart desired sooner rather than later.

The last thing I wanted was for Macy *not* to accept the offer in London, then hate me, grow resentful toward me later. Especially given the fact she'd already lost out on an even more amazing opportunity with *Hot Shot,* the guilt of knowing that slicing deep.

Strategies come with risks, gambles you place, hoping for the best outcome, and in the process, someone could end up hurt. My strategic mind strongly believed if I let Macy go, she'd be back since I knew we were meant to be. She just needed someone to give her wings to fly, a push, a reason to explore her opportunities as I had mine.

"You're not going home to Macy this weekend?" AJ packed his tattered UCLA duffle bag—the one he should have already replaced with a brand-new NY Jets duffle bag—with pants, shorts, socks, and his tablet.

I plopped onto the couch inside our hotel suite, located on training campgrounds, and pointed the remote to the television. "Nope, just gonna hang out with Damian for the weekend."

He scoffed. "Dude, don't tell me you're still trying to get Macy to hate you? Because hanging out with that prick, well, I may just end up hating you."

AJ knew what I'd been up to and while he had no problems telling me how sadistic the plan seemed to him, he still supported me as my bro. I mean, AJ was the guy you called to help you bury a body in the woods.

"Pretty sure Macy's already writing her 'I Hate Lucas Stone' song."

He tossed a pair of dirty socks at me. "Well, good luck with that, dude. I hope you know what the fuck you're doing. I'm headed to Nebraska to visit my parents and bring Sage home."

Partying with Damian was exhausting. The man loved women, fast cars, and drinking, things I got out of my system during years one and two of college. We mostly hung out in Atlantic City casinos. Gambling. Drinking. Dancing. Groupies hounded us, hounded me.

"Lucas Stone." Some curly-haired blonde sat down beside me at a casino bar. She was in a dress short enough to call a tank top, and too much makeup for my taste. "Me and my girlfriends have a suite and a bed with your name on it."

She crossed her leg, dress hiking up high enough to show she was probably wearing no underwear. It reminded me of the last time me and Macy had sex, after she'd worn that dress to the Ball.

I steered clear of the curly-haired slut, having no interest in being the jerk who cheated.

Damian had already earned a media-worthy reputation as a playboy, so paparazzi followed us around like dogs chasing bitches in heat, snapping pics left and right, Damian seemingly enjoying every moment.

～

THE WEEKEND ENDED AS FAST as it came.

"How do you stand this lifestyle?" I asked as we returned back to training campgrounds Sunday night.

Damian shrugged. "What? All the beautiful women?"

I nodded. "Partying all night. A different woman in your bed every night. All the drinking."

He laughed, slapping me on my back. "You only live once, my man."

Macy had called over a dozen times. Texted me about five times that amount, each text, each call going ignored.

When I realized she'd left a voicemail after one of those calls, I readily listened to it before going to bed.

Lucas? Thanks to TMZ Live, I've seen you out and about, partying like you've got no woman, no fiancée, no best friend at home wondering what the fuck she did to make you crush the heart you so eagerly wanted to hold in your hands.

Her words, the sobs in between, were a kick in the balls, the burn climbing up from my gut all the way to my throat, promising to choke me for what I'd done.

Fuck. Me.

THE WEEK LEADING up to next weekend trailed by.

Our camp schedule was insane, brutal as all hell.

Oatmeal and eggs for breakfast every day? Yeah, it sucked, and most mornings I was too beat up and sore to even want to shove food into my mouth.

Then it was mandatory that we head to the training room for treatment on all the injuries, if any, suffered the day before.

After that, weight lifting, which made me glad AJ and I took to lifting before camp.

Post-workout, there were meetings with the coach, and since I was a quarterback, I had the pleasure of attending our own meeting with team coordinators.

After all that, the physical practice took place, the first part going over plays discussed in the earlier meetings, followed by all the gridiron glory of acting like a bunch of gladiators out for blood.

By Friday night, I was banged up and beat, with no interest in spending another weekend partying like a rockstar.

I wanted to go home, wanted to see Macy.

By the time I got there, she was gone, and on the kitchen counter, her ring and a note with two words that shook my soul.

I'm done.

38

C onfessions of a Bookaholic

REVIEW *of My Personal Love Story: 1.5 Stars*

Love burns holes in the hearts of the innocent; the holes in mine are now permanent scars, reminders to always guard your heart.

I'm done with Lucas Stone, the drool-worthy morsel of hunky-hotness everyone read about when I accidentally published my digital diary online almost a year ago.

Done with him ignoring my calls.

Done with seeing him sprinkled all over TMZ riding the JockStar Express.

Done with Mr. Money Bags, the NFL's Most Valuable Prick.

Just. Done.

Shame on him for treating me like some throwaway hussy.

Shame on me for still wanting to get lost in his touch, his kisses, his love—but no one gets to fuck my heart up the way he did.

Mind made up, I'm on my way to London, England, shuffled away to the airport by Cosmo's *luxury car service, waving goodbye to all the broken promises of forever, goodbye to the idea of happy endings, goodbye to romance books and their stupid too-good-to-really-ever-exist book boyfriends, goodbye to false hopes. My personal love story gets 1.5 stars.*

This is my last blog entry.

Why? As you all may recall, I've shamelessly compared all book boyfriends to Lucas Stone, and seeing how I'd rather imagine a block of cheese instead of him, I need to step away from reading and reviewing, step away while I embark on this new chapter in my life, step away while I mend a tragically broken heart...

Take care of yourselves, my book besties,

Macy Sinclair, Former Romance Bookaholic

39

*L*ondon, England
Two Weeks Later
"This is where we keep all the bloody file folders and rubbish we rarely use anymore since most things are stored digitally." Oliver, the lead assistant to the Social Media Director was giving me a rundown on all things *Cosmopolitan,* London.

Tall and incredibly handsome, he trekked fast as I struggled to keep up, spoke with a strong cockney accent, and wore a tight, muscle-hugging button-down with a different color bow tie every day.

"And do not, I repeat, do *not* ever put anything that is not almond milk in her tea"—he leaned in, lowering his high-pitched voice an octave—"because she will shit her knickers, literally."

"Oh," I said, face heating, taking copious notes as we sprinted through the large office space. "And what about her lunch order again? Salad with or without dressing?"

Giving me a sideways glance, Oliver halted his tracks, chin raised high. "I usually make it a habit *not* to repeat myself, expecting fresh blood to keep up with my flow." He turned to face me, eyeing me up and down. "But I like you, Blondie. Feel like we could be mates."

"Mates?"

He rolled his eyes. "Bloody Americans. *Friends*, okay? Mates, as in friends. Anyway, on her salad"—he paused, flicking his gaze to pencil and pad in my hand—"you'll want to write this down." He waited until he saw me scribbling. "Dressing on the side, two croutons, four dried cranberries, and six pieces of baked chicken breast...diced."

"Right. Got it," I said, wanting to die.

It was my first full week and there was so much to learn. How to answer the phones, who was who, where to go for tea and coffee orders—all when I struggled to remember how to get from my tiny corporate-owned apartment to the office most days, which is sad considering it was just around the corner.

"Anyway," he said, motioning for me to follow. "Poppy Wright hates imperfection. So, the way to see she's happy is to make sure everything is perfect. Now, today, I'll leave it up to you to fetch her salad." He flashed a plastic smile that faded almost instantly. "Best of luck."

"Right. Cool. Thanks."

~

"I ASKED FOR EXTRA CRANBERRIES. Can't you get *anything* right?"

Poppy Wright glared at me as she moved her fork through the baked chicken and cranberry salad on her desk.

Five weeks in, and I still couldn't seem to get her damn lunch order right, although in my defense, she changed it every day—wanting four cranberries one day and a dozen the next.

Only a few years older than me, she was tall, ebony-haired, with cheekbones that could cut glass. No kidding, she was drop-dead gorgeous, with a delicious British accent, and always wore short skirts and dresses—barely-there eye-popping garments that seemed to make everyone in the office swoon. But she had a bad case of Crazy Bitch, and people in the office often compared her to Miranda Priestly. Cold. Mean. Insensitive. And as she stared up at me, nose flaring, something inside me snapped.

"Perhaps if you'd just learn not to be so picky and stopped randomly switching your order up each day...then, you know, you'd see I do get things quite right."

Green eyes wide, she looked as though I'd just presented her a first-class ticket to hell. "I don't know how people speak to their bosses back in America, but here, your tone is unacceptable." She surveyed me up and down. "You can go home for the day, come back tomorrow with your tail between your legs."

Verdict was in.

Cosmopolitan, London sucked.

MY ADVICE TO EVERYONE IS, don't try to nurse a broken heart while living far away from friends and family. Nights at home were bad; they were when I missed Lucas the most.

Lonely evenings filled with Netflix and no chill, I found myself scrolling through photos of us on my phone, reading ESPN about his game stats, and streaming games when I could find them. Shit, I even watched TMZ to see if I'd catch a photo someone had snapped of him with another woman, but there were none. In fact, other than those few photos that had popped up of him partying with Damian during training camp, nothing had popped up of Lucas since. I rushed to work early most days. The torture from Poppy was far better than being home, trying to piece together the events that led to a breakup that felt like I had swallowed shards of glass that ultimately pulverized my heart.

Sage and Chloe always seemed out of reach due to the time

difference, but there were rare occasions I was able to catch them both on FaceTime.

"I miss you guys."

"Then come back, you bitch," Sage said, sobbing. "You're missing out on the many stages of my belly growth."

Chloe rolled her eyes. "You can barely tell she's pregnant still."

"How's *Cosmo?*" Sage asked, her face noticeably more round.

"I hate it. Nothing I dreamed of. Plus, my boss is the devil who walks around in short, skimpy dresses, barking about salad orders."

Chloe deadpanned. "So, instead of your boss being The Devil Wears Prada, your boss is The Devil Wears Nada?"

We all laughed our asses off.

"But for real, you should just come home and stay with me and AJ, so you don't run into..." Sage stopped talking, knowing she was never to say *his* name again. "Well, I just miss my best friend."

Chloe scoffed. "I always knew she loved you more than me."

Truth is, I wanted to go home, wanted to run into Lucas and yell, kick, and scream. Tell him I hated that my love for him was a waste—love spent recklessly, love neither of us could get back.

The three of us chatted for a few minutes more before hanging up and promising to video chat at least three times a week.

"Love you, Macy," they both said.

"Love you guys, too."

$\sim$

PISSED OFF ABOUT LIFE, I headed to the local pub. But the annoying thing about living so close to where I worked was the fact I couldn't go to the pub without bumping into someone from the office, like Oliver. Ugh.

"Are you pissed?" he said, plopping down onto the bar stool beside me, head atilt as he assessed me.

I nodded, guessing the brokenhearted angry scowl I'd been wearing on my face had become a permanent fixture. "Yep. Every single day."

He asked the bartender for a beer. "Explains a lot, like how you always manage to fuck up Poppy's salad."

I rolled my eyes.

"Where do you keep your stash?"

I glared at him, cockeyed. "My...*stash*?"

"That bottle of water, you chug." He elbowed me, cackling. "Not quite water, is it?" He winked.

Lost, I said, "I honestly do not know what you're talking about."

"Right. I suspect Dave in Fashion Merch does the same thing as you." He took a swig of his beer. "I mean, how else would the chap be able to walk around looking so chipper all the time? I think he spikes his tea. Whiskey perhaps."

"Wait." I laughed. "You think I *drink* at work?"

"Well, you just told me you're pissed every day, right?"

I laughed again. "Pissed to me means that I'm angry or upset. Pissed to you means...?"

"Drunk. Three sheets to the fucking wind." He released a guffaw. "Shit's hilarious. Here I thought you'd been knocking back vodka hidden in bottled water at work." Dark brown eyes assessed me again. "What's got you feeling angry, or sorry, your version of *pissed,* every day?"

I shrugged. "I'm not sure I know the difference between sad and angry anymore. They are starting to feel the same."

"Guy trouble?"

I nodded, taking a sip from my wineglass.

"Been there. Done that, mate. In fact, the last guy who broke my heart is a bloke from New York City. I met and fell in love with him when I worked there. Tall, dark, and annoyingly handsome."

I giggled. "Sounds like my Lucas. Well, he used to be *my* Lucas."

"What happened?"

"Wanna know the long version or short version?"

He ordered me another glass of wine and then another beer for himself. "I'll take the long version, please."

An hour later, I'd spilled mostly all details about Lucas, from our first playdate to our last, tear-filled sobs in between. I even told him about how I'd lost the opportunity at *Hot Shot* and that I only took the job at *Cosmo* because it provided me an immediate escape from the hurt.

Oliver took a few minutes to process all I'd shared.

He patted my shoulder. "While I sure as shit do not view myself as an expert in happily-ever-afters, it sounds like your story has not quite come to its end, not from how you explained your relationship over the years." He finished off his beer, the bottle hitting the counter with a thud. "And regarding *Hot Shot,* remember how I said I used to live in New York?"

I gulped my wine and bobbed my head in acknowledgment.

"Well, mate, Kat Agassi was my boss back then. *Hot Shot* was my first ever magazine job. She's super sweet and easy to talk to. We're still friends today."

"Why did you leave New York? Leave *Hot Shot?*"

"That guy that broke my heart is supermodel Jake Agassi, Kat's brother."

My mouth practically fell into my lap.

"I had to get away, so I fled back here, landing a job at *Cosmo,* thanks to Kat who put in a good word. *Hot Shot* and *Cosmo* are operated under the same corporate umbrella."

"Big world. Small world," I said finishing off the last sip of my wine.

"Indeed it is, my friend."

Oliver became my ally after that night, and miraculously,

Poppy Wright got off my back, too, even though I managed to get her stupid salad order wrong no matter what I did.

But I still hated *Cosmo*. Still missed my friends back home. Still ached for Lucas.

Weeks rolled by, and shit got crazy as the magazine prepared for its most anticipated issue.

Editors in Chief from other magazines were expected for the annual Fall Issue Townhall Meeting, and the last person I'd expected to bump into caught me off guard in the ladies restroom.

"Well, if it isn't Macy Sinclair." Kat Aggasi smiled at me through the bathroom mirror, dazzling white teeth a picture-perfect contrast to her beautifully tanned skin. She was effortlessly stylish in a formfitting designer suit.

In her presence, my mouth suddenly forgot how to speak so I simply smiled.

"I heard you joined *Cosmopolitan,* which was somewhat comforting considering I'd wondered where you disappeared to." She dabbed a thin layer of red lipstick on. "Nonetheless, I take it you're happy here?"

I gave a one-shoulder shrug, still unable to speak real words.

"Well, I had big plans for you." She tossed her lipstick into her clutch, then turned around to face me. "Much more than being an assistant, so if ever you find yourself back in New York, you know where to find me."

40

LUCAS

"Nice game, Lucas." Coach patted me on the back as my teammates gave me high-fives.

Another win under the belt. Go Jets.

I poured everything I had into football, considering there was nothing else left.

Macy was my everything and I was stupid enough to push her away instead of just talking to her.

What the fuck was I thinking?

Oh, right.

That if I let her go, fate would bring her back to me.

Well, fuck fate. I should have just talked to her about the job. But, I figured Macy would have still given up her shot, too afraid the distance between us would somehow break our love. And now look at us, shattered into pieces anyway.

I never thought I could miss someone so much, could ache for someone so much, could cry for someone so much.

Photos of us still clung to the walls of the house meant for two, and I swear, months later, and I could still smell her perfume in our bedroom.

Nights were the loneliest. And the closer I got to the date we were supposed to tie the knot, the more my heart threatened to shatter inside my chest.

I dialed and texted her number countless times and it wasn't until some dude with some weird accent answered that I realized she'd changed her number.

I wanted—needed—to win her back, and while I wasn't sure how, my ass was going to be on a flight to London during my teams next bye week.

Being new to the NFL, reporters were stalking me left and right for interviews—most of them I'd turned down.

But when my agent reached out and said *Hot Shot* wanted to speak to me, my ears perked up.

"They're doing a piece on some of the sexiest players in the NFL. The editor-in-chief, some hottie named Kat Agassi, asked for you specifically."

Though reluctant, I agreed, trusting a gut feeling.

When I arrived at *Hot Shot* headquarters, women whispered and giggled as I was led by a tall, male receptionist with pink, spiky hair to a glass-enclosed office, its floor-to-ceiling windows overlooking Central Park.

"Mrs. Agassi? I've got Lucas Stone."

He motioned for me to step in and when I did, the blonde behind the large, off-white desk invited me to take a seat.

Easing down onto the high-back chair in front of her desk, I bounced my leg, checking out the hundreds of photos of past issues plastered to the walls—some of which I'd recognized that Macy had read. The memory of her curled up on our couch, nose all in *Hot Shot's Please Your Man* issue, made me chuckle.

"Something funny, Mr. Stone?"

I shook my head. "Oh, my fiancée—well, I guess my ex-fiancée —used to read *Hot Shot* when we were in college. Seeing all these past issues on the walls made me think of how she used to be very into some of the"—I trailed off to find my words—"more popular issues."

Kat nodded, her lips pursed. "Are you talking about Macy Sinclair?"

Perplexed, I said, "Yes, I am, why?"

She sat up in her chair, finger tapping her chin. "Macy is one of the reasons why I requested this meeting with you." She exhaled. "See, Mr. Stone—"

"Lucas. Please, call me Lucas," I interjected, feeling the need to stop her because anytime I heard a woman say, Mr. Stone, my mind conjured up thoughts about Macy. She'd always call me that during her sassiest moments.

I wouldn't call my birthday suit nothing, Mr. Stone... My lips curved up at the memory.

"Okay, Lucas, then," Kat went on. "Anyway, I ran into her in London last week and, well..." She paused, lifting up a printed sheet of paper. "I should probably first ask if you've read her last *Confessions of a Bookaholic* blog entry she posted about two months ago?"

My brows drew together. "No, I must have missed that post." Macy had deactivated the app not too long after what she always called bloggergate.

She reached over, handed me the sheet of paper. "Here you go. Read this, then we'll finish our talk."

I took the paper, my eyes giving perusal over words Macy must have written the day she left for London.

Love burns holes in the hearts of the innocent; the holes in mine are now permanent scars, reminders to always guard your heart...

My stomach burned, scorched by the pain she evidently felt, my throat suddenly closing.

Kat stood up, walked over to her window. "Now, I don't know what you did to make her feel so obviously heartbroken, but my question to you is, do you want her back?"

I coughed, trying to get my emotions in check. "Of course, I want her back. I'm leaving for London in three days, though I have no idea what I'm going to do."

Kat spun around, walked back to her desk, and claimed her chair. "Let me help you." She rocked back, confidence etched into her face. "Women like Macy, who've read novel after novel of pages filled with romance, won't be easily wooed by a guy who just shows up."

"Okay, you've got my attention."

"For her, a simple grand gesture won't suffice. Macy is going to need something unexpected, the perfect ending, or beginning, depending on how you look at it, to her love story."

I crossed my arms over my chest. "What's in it for you?"

"I had offered Macy a job here last year, a pretty high-end position. My offer still stands, but somehow she ended up at *Cosmo,* and since they're one of our sister magazines, Legal won't let me recruit her."

"Okay, what does that have to do with me?"

Kat picked up a mock-up of her magazine. "Two birds. One stone. Win. Win."

She went on to explain that *Hot Shot* was prepared to publish an exclusive public love letter of apology from me to Macy in response to her last blog post.

"A love letter? From me? A jock?"

"Yes." Her eyes glittered with excitement. "The headline will say something like, *Romancing The Playbook. One of the NFL's Sexiest Players Proves Romance Isn't Dead.*"

I felt intrigued, but not convinced. "How will I know my public letter will land on Macy's eyes?"

"Simple. The gentleman who Macy works closely with at *Cosmopolitan* is a close friend. He'll see that she gets a copy."

41

September thirteenth.

One month before my birthday. One month before my planned nuptials.

I was in a pisspot mood.

Hating *Cosmopolitan.*

Hating London.

Hating the rain that made my hair frizzy.

Hating that I missed Lucas Stone.

Sitting at my desk, sifting through too many emails, I decided I needed coffee, not the crap tea everyone around me seemed to drink.

Texting Oliver to let him know I was going on a coffee run, he hopped over to my desk, looking too happy-go-luckyish for a day I classified as Friday, the Shiteenth.

"Actually, I need you to be at your desk in about two minutes. Very important communication being sent out to the staff about..." He trailed off as if stuck in his own head. "Carats."

"Carrots?"

"Mmhmm." He stroked his ring finger then nodded curtly. "Carats."

Freaking Cosmo *weirdos.* I breathed a puff of air out of my mouth, wondering why a magazine felt the need to distribute something about a root vegetable. "Okay then. I will sit here at my desk and wait for the all-important staff memo regarding carrots."

"*Carrrrats,*" he repeated, as if I were hard of hearing, striking not just one, but all of my patience nerves.

"Right," I huffed. "Carrots."

Seriously, if he repeated the word one more fucking time, my hand was ready to slap him.

He sauntered over to his desk across from mine and sat down humming, *Can You Feel The Love Tonight.*

I wanted to heave.

Minutes later a ping notified me of a new email in my inbox.

"Email for you," Oliver singsonged.

"Great," I said under my breath. "Let's see this memo about carrots, shall we?"

Oliver coughed out, "Carats."

Ugh.

Inside my inbox was an email from Oliver that said, "Open Now."

When I did, it was an email forwarded to him from Kat Agassi, Hot Shot magazine that said, "This went live on our site today."

Curious, I clicked the link.

Then basically died.

The link took me to a spread in *Hot Shot* magazine, a picture of a handsomely suited-up—God, he looked so delicious—Lucas Stone, posing on bended knee, holding a ring—my ring—and lined up beside the photo was a heart-melting letter, *a love letter* addressed to me.

ROMANCING THE PLAYBOOK: *An Open Love Letter From One of the NFL's Sexiest Players Proves Romance Isn't Dead*

. . .

DEAR MACY,

Sixteen years ago, I walked over to your house, conjuring up the nerve to press my knuckles against the door and knock. I must have stood at your door for God knows how long before finally taking a deep breath and knocking.

Even at six years old, I thought you were the prettiest girl I'd laid my eyes on, dazzling me with your missing-front-teeth smile, freckle-crested nose, and golden ponytails.

I asked your father if he'd let you play outside with me and when he said yes, I took your hand in mine, and since that day, I've never wanted to let go.

Until I had to.

I'd always hated the cliché saying that suggests if you love someone, set them free. I never put much thought into its significance.

But when I realized the woman I loved would probably put her own dreams on hold while I actively pursued mine, I couldn't sit back and let that happen.

Knowing she wouldn't accept an amazing out-of-the-country opportunity on her own, I purposely devised a strategy—a dim-witted one, mind you—to push her away. I became the biggest dick alive, so she'd become frustrated enough to leave, go after her own dreams, without feeling guilty about leaving me behind.

Only my plan backfired because I ended up hurting her—hurting you, Macy Sinclair—in ways unimaginable.

The last couple of months have been torture without you, I've been a prisoner of this mess I created, and can only imagine what these months have been like for you.

I can't breathe.

I can't sleep.

I can't eat.

I can't dream.

I can't be...without you.

Because I love you.

So, though you're miles away, I wanted to tell you I'm sorry for being a jerk. Sorry for hurting you. Sorry for making you think love stories don't exist, when in fact, ours is, in my opinion, the greatest ever told. I pray you'll forgive me.

And today, I am openly proposing to you just as I did a few months ago before I messed all of this up...

No one else will ever hold my heart, love me, the way you do, and I promise, no one will hold your heart, adore, appreciate, and protect you the way I do.

Seems from day one we've been a love story in the making, and this ring will guide us toward our happily-forever-after.

Let's hold our hearts in each other's hands for life.

Macy Sinclair, marry me, baby.

Please.

IT HAD BEEN weeks since a smile found my lips, his beautiful words holding all of me captive, dead heart finally beating again.

Butterflies break-dancing in my chest, I heard a very familiar, "Hey," that sent my heart cartwheeling to the moon.

Spinning around, my eyes caught sight of Lucas Stone standing two feet behind me, holding a ring box, wearing a chest-hugging silk tee, and a pair of cock-enhancing jeans I wanted to yank off.

Hands over face, I melted, boohooing, not caring that mascara was all over my face, or that the entire office staff came from behind their desks to watch the next few minutes unfold.

"Hey," I finally replied, a giggle bubbling free.

Walking over to where I was sitting, Lucas got down on one knee and flashed a smile that could heal a thousand love-shattered hearts.

He cupped my face, the minuscule contact a reminder that his touch alone set my whole body on fire. "I've waited my whole life to have you, and I swear if you marry me, I'm never letting you go. Please marry me, baby."

I flashed a smirk, knowing it made him all sorts of crazy. "Give me one reason why, Mr. Stone."

He pulled me close, our lips only a scrape away. "Because, Macy Sinclair, I promised you forever."

42

One Month Later

Lucas: Hey, meet me in the hallway.

I eyeballed my future husband's text message, fighting back a grin. Why he'd asked for a meeting in the hallway twenty minutes before the start of our wedding, was beyond me.

Me: Why? You know you can't see me before the wedding.

"Look up," Chloe barked, giving my mascara its final touch-up. "Unless you want to walk down the aisle with raccoon eyes."

"Aren't raccoon eyes a thing, now?" Sage quipped, as she sat on the dressing room sofa, fanning herself. Two weeks past her due date, she'd been hot and cranky all morning.

"Not for a wedding," Chloe retorted with a side-eye glare that could part the Red Sea. "Although Macy would probably make raccoon eyes at her wedding look amazing."

My phone vibrated with another text from the groom.

Lucas: I know, baby. But I need to give you something.

Per usual, my cock-struck ass had its mind in the gutter.

Me: Mr. Stone, you'll have the whole night to give me...something.

"Macy..." Chloe scolded, brandishing the mascara wand around my face like a sword. "Be. Still."

Another text came in, and I held my phone up to read the message.

Lucas: I'm happy I get to marry a sex kitten in twenty minutes. But, seriously. I need to give you something. It's to go with your 'something old'.

I'd waited forever to marry this man; do you think I was about to mess with luck and forfeit traditional wedding rules?

Uh, no.

It was bad enough we almost had to postpone our nuptials, afraid we wouldn't be able to plan an elaborate three-hundred-fifty guest wedding in less than a month. Yet, thankfully, neither one of us cancelled the venue, and Kat Agassi—my new boss—had a long list of contacts we were able to call on.

"I'll send Sage out instead."

Hobbling like a warthog, my extremely pregnant best friend made her way out to the hallway while Chloe finished applying my mascara.

"Swear to God, if only I had a needle to pop her, then that baby will probably fly right out of her," Chloe whispered.

"Just so long as no baby flies out of her today."

Chloe laughed. "Instead of tossing the bouquet..."

Sage waddled back, plopping onto the couch breathless. "I can hear you, Chloe. Your so-called *whispers* can wake the mother humping dead." She was back on her cleanse, once again using partial placeholders after having fallen off the potty-mouth wagon more than enough times.

Hand extended, I asked Sage to give me the small envelope she was now fanning herself with. "Isn't that what Lucas wanted you to give me?"

"Sorry," she huffed, motioning for Chloe to retrieve it. "I'm losing my mind with the baby and all these F-word Braxton Hicks contractions."

"Which is why Lucas and I told you and AJ it would be just fine if you had decided to stay home today."

As I opened the envelope Chloe passed me, a silver necklace fell out and onto my lap.

A small gasp escaped my lips, mesmerized by the jewelry shimmering in the light as it dangled on my finger.

"What's that?" Chloe asked, applying blush to her naturally defined cheekbones.

Shrugging, I said, "Not sure," palming the beautiful pendant, the shape of a broken heart, to read its inscription, which at closer glance said, *Lucas*.

Baffled, I was about to ring Lucas, but he beat me to it, prompting me to answer on the first ring.

"Hey," I began, "you're giving me a broken-heart pendant on our wedding day?"

He laughed. "No, baby. It's a necklace I planned to give you for your thirteenth birthday."

"Ten years ago?"

"Yep. Hence the 'something old'."

"Okay? I don't get it."

"See, I was going to give it to you until we made that stupid pact to forever be best friends. You were to have the half of the heart with my name on it and I was to have the half with your name on it." He cleared his throat. "Point being I was into you then, wanted to ask you to be my girlfriend. Instead, we had the fight that led to the pact sending my plan straight to hell."

Tears pricked my eyes, and I willed them to stay put or I'd really be walking down the aisle with raccoon eyes. "You've had this the whole time?"

"Well, kind of. Mom found them tucked away in her jewelry

box this morning. I'd forgotten all about giving them to her to hold, back then."

I hit the jackpot. I mean, the man was like a kickass gift you'd never think about regifting.

"I love you, Mr. Stone."

"I love you, too, almost Mrs. Stone. Tuck that something old in your dress and get your sexy-as-all-hell ass out here and marry me."

THE PEWS at Cathedral Basilica were bedecked with tulle bows, my body shaking as Dad led me down the aisle with a custom runner that said, *Lucas and Macy Forever Ever After.*

Speaking of forever, it seemed to take an eternity to reach my groom, the wedding march seemingly much longer than it had been during all the rehearsals just days before.

Friends and family let out audible oohs and ahhs as I sauntered by, familiar faces gushing at me from left and right.

Approaching the altar, I kept my attention glued to members of the wedding party: Sage, who was rubbing her belly, and Chloe, my two Maids of Honor; and AJ, my handsome groom's Best Man, while they all watched, eyes twinkling, as I drew near. I knew if I'd taken one look at Lucas, I would have started the tear fest way too soon.

Even so, once my dad and I reached the altar, Lucas captured my gaze with his sweet baby blues, a smile that truly did melt my panties, and a tux that glorified his all-muscle body.

Hands in his, I prayed my mouth would not lose the ability to talk.

"Hey," he said, face beaming.

"Hey," I said right back, prompting our wedding guests to erupt in giggles.

The priest began his spiel and it felt like no one was in the church but me and my man. Vows we'd written were exchanged, rings slid onto fingers—and the moment I'd been waiting for, since I picked up my first Danielle Steel novel, arrived.

"I now pronounce you husband and wife. You may kiss the—"

"Holy, S-word," Sage yelped. "My water! My water just effing broke.

And as the saying goes, good things come to those who wait.

Sage and AJ waited two weeks past their due date for their baby, a sweet and healthy little guy they named Andrew Jackson, Jr. who was born on my birthday, the day I finally married the man of my bookaholic dreams...

Lucas Stone, the drool-worthy morsel of hunky-hotness who'd been my best friend since forever.

EPILOGUE

LUCAS

Five Years Later
Lucas
Hot. Wife.

Those two words had pretty much been the everlasting definition of Macy Stone, my breathtakingly beautiful-as-all-hell best friend, lover, and wife.

After our heartbreaking—and thankfully short-lived—separation five years ago, Macy and I vowed to communicate more effectively, to never let assumptions guide any of our decisions. We had both been temporarily blinded by thinking we knew what was best for the other person, when it all could have been avoided if we took time out of our own heads. It was a hard lesson learned but one we—myself especially—ultimately grew from.

I thanked God for Macy.

Every. Single. Day.

Our first five years as husband and wife had been nothing but bliss—all that spicy banter, sass and steaming hot sex included—and I was ready for fifty more years times infinity.

My football career had been one made of dreams, too, winning two Super Bowl championships, and MVP—ahem—

Most Valuable Player. The Jets extended my contract, as did major sponsors like Nike, and I was in talks with ESPN to be a commentator once I finally decided to hang up my cleats.

Macy thrived working for *Hot Shot, Confessions of a Bookaholic* soaring to levels unimaginable as one of the magazine's most read contributions. Her fanbase grew even larger, and the app that prompted me to read her tell-all confessions was re-activated—yes, I was one of the first to resubscribe.

Life was some kind of amazing.

Until, *wham!*

An out of nowhere—*seemingly intentional*—diary post, from Macy that turned our life into some kind of spectacular.

DEAR DIGITAL DIARY,

What do you give a man who's given you the world?

Well, how about a little slice of heaven he'll get to hold in his arms nine months from now...

THE END.

DEAR FABULOUS READERS!

Thank you for reading CONFESSIONS OF A BOOKAHOLIC!!

I hope you enjoyed Lucas and Macy's story as much as I enjoyed writing it!!

CONFESSIONS OF A BOOKAHOLIC had been in my heart for over two years before it finally began to come to life at the start of the Covid-19 Pandemic—when my writing got put on hold as we adjusted to the new normal and changed schedules to accommodate home-schooling and working from home. But thanks to sleepless nights, I was able to craft Macy and Lucas's journey to their well-deserved HEA.

Friends-to-lovers has always been one of my favorite tropes, even more so when the two are lifetime friends.

Sage and AJ were such fun side characters, and my plan was to write a book about them as well...

Who knows? Maybe I will. :-)

ACKNOWLEDGMENTS

Thank you to all of my author friends who I look up to. Roberta, Julie, Arell, and Terra—you are all amazing!! XO

Thanks to Jen at Wildfire Marketing for your help and amazing support! I am truly thankful!

Thanks to Opium House Creatives for the fabulous cover.

Ashli M. and Nadine P. - Thank you for being my awesome beta readers as I tossed you a chapter at a time or several chapters at a time.

My Editors: Kathy you have no idea how valued you are and how I SO appreciate you coming through for me at the last minute (literally) to help make this book shine. THANK YOU!!! And also Amy who first tackled the manuscript, giving her touch of sparkle before it went to Kathy.

Tandy Proofreads - thank you!!!

My Hubby - I LOVE YOU...but you know this!!!

My Kids - LOVE YOU! XO

ARC Team - Thank you all for taking time out of your busy lives to read the ARC and for offering all the feedback! Your support is everything to me!!

Bloggers - I Love You ALL!

A special thanks to Rachela Farella for coming up with Harper Kingston's name.

A special thanks to Heather Breyer for coming up with Bare Kitten, the lingerie boutique.

Thank you to my A-Listers Facebook Group - you all make me smile!

XO Joslyn

CINDERELLA-ISH SNEAK PEEK

Chapter One - Daniella

You're a sweet, take-you-home-to-meet-my-mom type of a girl and I'm just not ready for something so serious.

The text message invades my phone like an unforeseen missile strike. Boom.

Is that the best Jacob Ryan could come up with? A pathetically buffed-up rendition of *it's not you, darling, it's me*?

A breakup text.

I've heard of them, yet seriously doubted I'd ever be on the receiving end of one.

You'd think I'd be hurt, right? Especially since Jacob and I've been dating for over a month. Forty-five days to be precise.

But I'm not hurt one bit.

Seriously.

I mean, I sort of gave up on meeting my *Prince Charming* ages ago. Mr. Charming does not exist and, believe me, every modern-day woman knows this, despite all of the sappy romance movies and novels out there.

So fuck it. I'm totally swearing off men now. Alpha men, hot men, poor men, rich men, short men, tall men...

Just men. Period. End of discussion.

And I mean it this time. I—Daniella Belle—do solemnly swear to *never* go out with another damn member of the opposite sex again. Ever.

Well, at least for now, anyway.

Never is a borderline extreme commitment that I'd surely fail to live up to. For example: Suppose Circa-2000 David Beckham were to strut across this busy Los Angeles Metro station platform wearing nothing except his ripped abs and jeans? He'd seductively squeeze his way through the crowd of downtown-bound commuters, his gaze glued to mine as he makes a beeline toward me, professing Victoria—what's-her-face—has left him and he wants to be with me. Then, of course, I'd forgo swearing off men.

Obviously.

Anyway, this epiphany-inducing text could not have come at a worse time. Today is *supposed* to be a great day. Yet already, my alarm clock failed to go off, I got shampoo in my eyes, there were no more Pop-Tarts in the pantry, and of course now, this gimpy-ass text.

When a day starts off bad, it has a tendency to only get worse. This theory has been statistically proven to be true, which instinctively compels me to internally pray to the good day gods that today does *not* snowball into an epic-fail-shit-happens sort of day. From this point on it's gotta be smooth mutha fuckin' sailing.

I'm on my way to a job interview that, if all goes as planned, will land me my dream job.

Well, my *almost* dream job. Let's just call this the get-my-foot-in-the-door-to-my-dream-job job. One that is, after all, the sole reason why I moved to Los Angeles from Dallas; to be a fashion designer—a designer of lingerie, to be more specific.

I graduated at the top of my class from LA's Fashion Institute of Design last year. Except so far, I've had zero luck getting anyone to notice my designs.

Budging my way through the crowd of busy Los Angeles commuters, I feel my phone's vibration through my purse.

I cringe.

It better not be another text from Jacob, the breakup texter.

I yank my phone out of my purse and peek at the caller ID.

Oh. It's my boss. Well, she's also a good friend. So what's the term for that? Boss slash friend?

"Hey, Stacy," I answer, slowly inching my way closer to the edge of the platform.

"Best of luck today, lovely. Have you caught the train yet?"

Stacy's actually the one who showed me the Google alert that mentioned: Antonio Michaels, Creator and CEO of *CraveMe Lingerie* is actively seeking a professional and experienced Personal Assistant.

Honestly, I had never even heard of Antonio Michaels. Sure I've heard of his *CraveMe* line of lingerie, but seriously...who hasn't?

"Not yet. Still waiting at the station. Along with a whole bunch of other people. I may have to fight my way onto the train." I laugh internally at my sarcasm.

"You can't be late for that interview. I don't want to lose you as a nanny to Emma, but you can't miss out on an opportunity so great."

True confession time: I've got no *real* experience being anyone's Personal Assistant; yet, Stacy swore that, since I've been a nanny to her daughter Emma, I've really been like her Personal Assistant over the past five years, basically keeping her entire professional world, as a lawyer, and personal world, as a single mom, organized.

Stacy helped me spruce up my résumé and gave me a respectable letter of recommendation. And a letter of recommendation from Stacy is full-on, drop-the-mic status, on account of she's a well-known entertainment lawyer.

"I won't miss the train. I promise. And thank you, Stacy. You're the best. Oh, and guess what? Jacob broke up with me." I pause and lower my voice after catching a woman in close proximity eavesdropping. "Via text," I add.

"What a loser!" Stacy announces as if it's breaking news. "I told you he doesn't deserve you. Anyway, I'm walking into court right now. Emma will be home briefly this afternoon before she heads to her dad's for the rest of the week."

I nod as if Stacy can see me.

"And I'm catching a red-eye to New York," she asserts.

I actually forgot about that. Even though I made all of her travel arrangements. She's off to some lawyers' convention for the week.

"Right. New York. Have fun!"

"Sure. Well, I'll catch up with you later. Good luck. Love ya."

"Love ya, too."

As the train approaches, I keep a careful eye out for anyone holding a coffee cup. The last thing I need is for someone to solidify this to be a bad day, by bumping into me and spilling coffee all over my new dress. Shit like that isn't just made for TV; it happens all the time.

The train reaches the platform and as soon as I board, I realize it's standing room only.

Figures.

These stilettos aren't really made for standing.

As I maneuver my way to the back of the train, hoping to find an empty seat, my phone buzzes.

Ugh. Another text from Jacob *the loser* Ryan.

Just checking: Did you get my text message this morning?

I roll my eyes in unbelievable disgust at his inquiry and am just about to text a scathing reply, letting him know exactly where he can shove his stupid-ass breakup text, when I trip over who knows what, and land right up against a tall, dark-haired guy who's eating—a jelly donut.

That's right a...Fucking. Jelly. Donut.

Never did I think I'd need to be on the lookout for anyone eating a fruity donut on the train. A donut that has left its explicit mark on the top half of the front of my brand-new sweater dress.

Did I mention it's a *white* dress?

"Whoops." The dark-haired guy snickers, as he continues to bite and annoyingly smack his way through his evil donut. He doesn't even look the least bit concerned with the fact that remnants of his shitty breakfast choice are now splattered across the top front of my dress as blatant as a large letter *S* for Superwoman.

I scoff at his nonchalant response and reach into my purse in search of something I can use to wipe off the massive glob of jelly.

"Whoops? That's all you've got to say?" I briefly consider getting my revenge by snatching what's left of the donut out of his hand and smearing it all over his light blue button-down dress shirt.

He produces a semi-wicked grin. "Well, it wasn't *my* fault. You do know you totally bumped into me, right? You really shouldn't be texting and walking. It's evidently impairing. In all actuality, I saved you."

I finally retrieve a tissue out of my purse. "I beg your pardon? You saved me?" I shake my head and roll my eyes. Surely he must know I'm annoyed.

"Yes. Had I not been standing here for you to clumsily bump into after you tripped, you would have epically face-planted your way to the floor of this train. So please...feel free to thank me anytime now."

Really? He can't possibly be serious, right? Where is this guy from: the land that time forgot?

"Oh, I'll thank you, alright. You, along with your fucking

donut, have ruined my dress *and* my day. I'm on my way to a job interview. Now *this* is how I'll be presenting myself. So if anything, thank you for ruining my day."

The train gives a swift jolt as it takes off, and of course, the movement forces me into Mister Not-So-Friendly which, ironically causes part of the glob of jelly to rub off my dress and onto his shirt.

Pushing myself off of him, I grab a tight hold of the pole and can't help but laugh at the sight of his shirt.

Sweet ironic revenge at its best.

He looks down at his shirt, then up at me. Without taking his eyes off me, he swipes the jelly off his shirt with the tip of his index finger, and calmly licks the sticky goo before he winks. "I've got a wide selection of clean shirts I can change into at my office."

For a split second, the sight of him licking his finger makes my spine tingle. The dark-haired guy is scrumptiously gorgeous—tall, tan, with smoldering blue eyes. But his sarcastic remark just downright infuriates me.

"You're a first-class jerk, aren't you?" I suggest, feeling my face heat up.

"Why would you say such a thing? You hardly know me." The tone of his voice has a delicate accent to it, a sultry brew of American, Italian, and French—an international delight, perhaps.

"Thank goodness for that," I admit. "I would pay good money to never have to bump into the likes of you again."

"Ouch. You certainly do possess a spicy little bite, huh? And a huge scruffy attitude, too." He flirts as he runs his tongue across his soft lips.

I glare at him, displaying I'm not at all interested in flirtatious banter. "Scruffy attitude? Let's not forget *you* are a huge reason why I have this attitude."

He shakes his head. "Oh no. Don't try to pin it on me. I watched you as you got onto the train. You looked annoyed after you glanced at your phone. And now you're taking it out on me. Let me take a wild guess...did someone dump you via text?"

"You know what? Screw you!" I spit out, more shocked than he probably is. Sure, I tend to curse like a sailor, but not in the presence of hundreds of commuters on a train.

"Whoa! Such language for a little lady." He smiles conspiratorially leaning in close enough for me to get an accurate count of the somewhat sexy sprinkle of freckles along the bridge of his nose. "Tell me, how many guys have you kissed with that potty mouth of yours?"

I step back, flabbergasted at his blatant audacity to deliver such a question so bluntly. Without much thought, I cleverly toss back, "Tell me, how many women have you lost with that endless arrogance of yours? It spills out of you with as much force as water gushing out of a busted water main."

As the train comes to a halt I realize it's my stop. At least I think it is.

I rush past the brute who has un-graced me with his presence for the last ten minutes, and as I get closer to the exit, I hear his voice gripe in the distance. "Good luck on that job interview, Miss Potty Mouth. It's a crying shame you can't use me as your character reference."

I've walked at least three blocks and, thankfully, I'm just about there. I was so flustered on the train, I got off a stop too soon. But who could blame me? The guy was utterly despicable. In my not so humble opinion, walking the rest of the way is a winning trade-off, despite the fact I know darn well my feet are going to be done-in by these shoes once I get to the office building for the interview.

Part of me wants to head back to Stacy's Beverly Hills home and forget this interview since my appearance is less than to be desired. Honestly, who shows up to an interview with food spillage? My gut tells me something good has got to come out of this bad start to my day. The worst is behind me...left on that train.

When I finally arrive, with about twenty minutes to spare, I head straight for the receptionist desk to check in and when I approach, a young woman popping pink bubble gum is busy on the computer. She bops her head from side to side as if she's got a groovy pop song stuck in there. At first glance, it's safe for me to assume she's around my age—early twenties, at least. Her dark blue eyes switch from the computer screen to my face, then almost immediately switch to the pitiful stain on my dress.

"Oh. My. Goodness! What happened to your beautiful dress, hon?" She covers her mouth and her eyes widen, displaying what appears to be empathetic shock.

Instinctively, I try to cover the now dried-up jelly glob with the palm of my hand, but realize it's a total waste of time.

"Oh, I was accosted by a jelly donut on the train this morning," I sarcastically explain.

"A jelly donut? That's freakishly bizarre because—" She pauses, holds up her index finger, and mouths the words 'hold on', reaching to answer the office phone that sits underneath a pile of file folders on her desk.

As she diverts her attention to the person on the other end of the phone, I take a seat on one of the two couches that sits in the center of the lobby. The black-and-white walls are decorated with large gold-framed photos of women who are scantily adorned in exquisite lingerie pieces—a tasteful shrine of blown-up magazine spreads of *CraveMe* unmentionables.

"Sorry about the interruption," the woman says, with a gesture for me to make a return to her desk. "The phone has been ringing nonstop since a job opportunity was announced." She looks at me questionably. "Wait. Are you here for an interview?" She steals a quick glance at my ill-stained dress again.

"Yes, actually I am."

"Oh, goody! What's your name, hon?"

"Daniella Belle. Belle with an E." I anxiously tap my fingernails against the top of her elongated, podium-style desk.

She picks up a clipboard and skims over the list of names. "Oh right, B-E-L-L-E. Here you are. Sign in, right next to your name, please. You're slotted for 9:53 a.m." She smiles as she hands me the clipboard along with an ink pen. "I'm Liza, by the way."

"It's great to meet you, Liza."

She focuses on me with her head cocked and her perfectly shaped eyebrows furrowed as I hand her the clipboard. "You look like you've had a rough start to your day. How about I loan you something to put over your dress? You know, to cover up that stain?"

"You'd do that for me?"

"Absolutely." She removes a beautiful hot-pink cashmere scarf hanging on the back of her swivel desk chair and hands it to me. "Here you go, sweetie. This should do the trick."

"Oh my! Are you sure it's okay?"

"Girl Scout's Honor. I would be beside myself if I didn't lend a helping hand. Besides, like I was about to mention just before the phone interruption, jelly donuts seem to be a—"

The phone rings again and this time, Liza mouths the words, "I'm so sorry."

I take the free moment to tie the scarf around my neck and let it hang slightly—just enough to cover the drastic stain.

Liza ends the call and informs me it's time for her to escort me to my interview. She places a telephone headset over her ears, maneuvers her way from around her desk, and motions for me to follow.

"This way, hon."

I follow close behind as we enter a hallway, accessible only via her keycard. Liza seems as sweet as she is stylish. She's wearing a cute black-and-white knee-length dress, black high-heeled pumps, and her blond hair is secured in a chic bun. She reminds me of a modern-day pinup girl.

Our walk down the hall comes to a halt as Liza points straight ahead. "Your interview will be right through those double doors. Just let me give you a brief rundown."

I nod, giving her my undivided attention as she leans against the bare wall.

"Okay, so as you know, Antonio Michaels is looking for a new Personal Assistant. He's insisted he conduct the interviews on his own and so far, out of maybe two dozen, he hasn't been the least bit impressed."

She looks at me puzzled, then in an almost motherly fashion, approaches me and pats down a piece of my hair that must look out of place.

"Anyhow," she continues, "just hand Antonio your résumé and let things progress from there. He's looking for some type of connection. Dottie, his last PA, retired last month. She's kind of got big shoes to fill because she had the ability to keep Antonio in line. He's kind of...well, I don't want to share too much more. It may make ya nervous."

"I'm not nervous. After the morning I had on the Metro, I'm feeling like nothing could be worse."

"You rode the Metro here this morning?" She checks her watch.

"Yep. But I got off the train too soon and walked about four blocks."

"You did appear to be a bit flustered when you approached my desk. Come on. You're up."

She leads the way, closer to the double doors, and I must admit, the anticipation of the unknown has surfaced.

What will this Antonio guy be like?

Will he have tough questions for me?

Will he scoff at my lack of PA experience?

We reach the double doors that, incidentally, look a lot larger now than they did ten seconds ago.

Liza smiles. "Funny thing," she says as she slowly turns the knob to open the door, "Antonio also had a jelly-donut-related incident on his way to work this morning. Maybe it's something you can use as an ice breaker? It may help you connect with him."

"Wait. What?" I almost stop in my tracks. "That's an odd coincidence. But a good enough ice breaker if you ask me," I say.

We enter the spacious office and right away, I can't help but notice the bay window that overlooks Downtown Los Angeles. The view is breathtaking—I could seriously get used to working in an office like this.

A tall, dark-haired, slender man in a dark blue suit is facing the large window with his hands securely nestled in the pockets of his perfectly creased slacks.

"Mr. Michaels? Your 9:53 interview is here," Liza says, then looks to me and whispers the words 'good luck' before making a quick exit.

"Just have a seat and I'll be right with you," he says, still facing the window.

I make my way toward one of the high-back chairs in front of what I assume is his desk.

He turns to walk toward the desk and our eyes lock. The look on his face is probably the same look fixed on my own—a look of unfathomable shock, although his is embellished with an impish grin.

"Well, well, well. If it isn't Miss Potty Mouth herself. *You're* my 9:53 interview?" says *Antonio Michaels*...formally known as the jelly-donut-eating, rude guy from the Metro.

And uh...someone better call in the cavalry; the bad day snow-ball has officially reached monumental avalanche status.

Chapter Two - Antonio

"You've got to be kidding me," grumbles the fiery woman I encountered earlier this morning on the Metro.

Truthfully, I hardly expected to see her again. Especially since I *never* take the Metro or any other form of public transportation. However, as part of our annual wager-fest, my buddy Jonah bet me a thousand bucks and a round of drinks that I'd never step foot on any form of Los Angeles public transportation.

So, for the first time—ever—I hastily embarked on a public transportation venture. I don't need the one-thousand dollars I'm set to earn from this wager. But I have yet to lose an annual bet. I simply hate losing...at anything.

Of course, Jonah was more than obliged to drop me off at the Metro station, saying he wanted to be sure I actually got on the train, making jokes as soon as I sat in his car.

"Dude," he began, "part of me wants to get on the train with you, hit record, and spread that shit all over YouTube, Snapchat, and Facebook. *No* one is gonna believe your prissy-perfecto ass is taking the Metro."

I flipped him the bird then adjusted the passenger seat of his Tesla to a comfortable reclining position. "Just shut up and drive. I don't wanna miss that train. And you, Sir-Jokes-A-Lot, should get prepared to pay the hell up. I'll take my thousand bucks divided up in crisp one-hundred-dollar bills. Please and thank you," I said with an insolent chuckle.

Jonah was certainly one to talk. He too has never taken public transportation. Being a product of money, he fits the bill of all clichés related to growing up in the 90210—Beverly Hills.

"I'll gladly pay up when the task has been fulfilled. By the way," he lightly punched my shoulder, "when are you gonna tell me what I have to do this year for wager-fest? You're like, way behind on that shit, man."

"I know. I've been busy planning *CraveMe's* contribution to the upcoming Fashion Show and Lingerie Ball. Man, with Dottie retiring, I've got my hands full. I'll think of something soon, even though it won't quite matter. You always lose."

Jonah grimaced at my comment, making me laugh in amusement. Then, I dutifully gave him a shoulder punch in return.

When we arrived at a stoplight, Jonah reached over to the backseat, then tossed me a small white paper bag. "Here you go. I was generous enough to buy you some breakfast."

I opened the bag and took a quick look inside. "Dude, really? Jelly donuts?"

"Fuck yeah. You might as well reward yourself for putting on your big-boy boxers by getting up the nerve to take the train." He let out an exaggerated laugh while covering his mouth with his hand. "I'm really surprised you made it *this* far. Shit, I might even pay you *two* thousand bucks."

"Oh, believe me, you'll pay up. Just be on time when you pick me up at my office later on today with payment in hand," I demanded.

"And will I get to see the beautiful Miss Liza? I'm telling you, that woman is so fucking fierce. I'd convince her to marry me *today* if she'd only talk to me," Jonah said, raising both eyebrows expressively. He's had a thing for my receptionist for the past two years. He just doesn't get that she'll probably never give him the time of day.

"Sorry, dude. Liza's just not that into you."

Jonah barreled into the Metro station like Speed-Racer 2.0, minutes before the train was due to arrive. "Oh, and come to think of it," I announced before closing the door of his shiny new Tesla. "I've got the perfect bet for you. I officially bet you a thousand bucks you'll get *no*where with Liza."

Jonah's jaw dropped and the dumbfounded look of shock that consumed his perfectly round face, was priceless.

By the time I boarded the train and took a seat, my stomach was growling like a ninja wolf. Despite the fact that a jelly donut would be the last thing I would ever indulge in, I reached into the bag, pulled one of those bad boys out, and bit right in. Before I knew it, the train took off. I found myself taking in the scenery, fascinatingly immersed in everyone around me. There were riders of all types: students, businessmen and women, a mixture of those who appeared to be homeless, touristy types, and those who looked like they just took the Metro to pass the time.

About twenty minutes later, the train came to a grinding halt, and as some jumped off, others hopped on. At this point in my train-riding endeavor, it was standing room only, and I graciously gave up my seat to a little elderly lady who was hauling groceries. She reminded me of my grandma back in Italy.

So anyway, I digress...

I moved toward the back of the train and parked myself up against a pole for support. I reached into the paper bag, removed the second donut, and took a hefty bite.

And *that's* when I saw her.

She appeared to be deep in thought, one hand clenched to the strap of her oversized designer bag, while the other hand was clenched to her cell phone. She carried herself with this naive, yet classy, allurement—as if she had no clue about her level of drop-dead-gorgeousness.

I tried, but couldn't take my eyes off of her and neither could those she eased past, most of them doing a double-take.

Her shiny black hair, long and straight, seemed to highlight her cappuccino-colored skin tone—a tone that made every revealing inch of her body look as though it had been personally kissed by the sun.

As if that wasn't enough, she wore an off-white sweater dress that tastefully clung to her body, showcasing an hourglass figure that would make Kim Kardashian's own curves gawk in envious admiration.

And icing on the cake: hot-pink five-inch stilettos that hoisted her petite body to a perfect-for-me height.

I swear, the woman was undoubtedly JDH.

Jaw. Dropping. Hot.

So there I was, all prepared to flash my Colgate smile as she walked by. But instead, as if in slow motion, she tripped on some guy's briefcase and landed up against me and that damn jelly donut.

It was a beyond epic fail moment—for her anyway. All I could manage to spill out of my mouth was the word, *whoops*. I meant no disrespect as I continued to eat my way through the rest of the donut—what else was I supposed to do? I had to get rid of it, right?

Her reaction was downright unexpected, catching me completely off-guard.

Why?

Because instead of thanking me and treating me like a hero for saving her from falling flat on her face, she scolded me.

That's right, she scolded *me*...Antonio Michaels.

And I found it annoyingly...sexy.

Sure, I probably could've been a tad sympathetic about how the red jelly from my donut left an extremely noticeable mark on the top half of her dress. But truth be told, the woman made me nervous.

No woman makes me nervous.

Anyway, she glared at me with those big green, cat-shaped eyes, and I almost melted. And don't let me begin to describe how good the woman smelled.

Yet, she proved to be quite a spicy little dish—armed with an attitude and a mouth that spit out cuss words as nonchalantly as a back-in-the-day baseball player spit out chewing tobacco.

Despite all of that, the potty-mouthed kryptonite-like woman has been renting the overly-crowded space in my mind ever since our encounter on the train. And now, like some unbelievably bizarre twist of fate, she's standing here.

In my office.

Looking even hotter than I remembered.

"*You're* Antonio Michaels?" She shakes her head and rolls her eyes, seeming to look a little disgusted.

I take slow, *I'm a cool guy* strides toward my desk, trying to shield how delighted I am to see her. "Yep. Last time I checked."

Don't be a dick. I internally remind myself.

She scoffs. "Of course you are. Look, I'm gonna save you the trouble and leave. Obviously, our impromptu meeting earlier would suggest we're *not* at all what one would consider to be working relationship material."

I see she's still armed with that saucy *bite me* coating.

With a sultry swing of her hair and one hand on her hip, she pivots and stomps out of my office.

Instinctively, I rush after her, but, like an idiot, I stumble over one of my oversized desk chairs. "Wait!" I call out; yet, like a swift flash of lightning, she darts completely out of sight.

By the time I reach Liza at the front receptionist desk, Miss Potty Mouth is nowhere to be seen.

Damn it.

"Antonio, is everything okay?" Liza asks, rising up from the seat behind her desk.

"Do you happen to know the name of my 9:53 interview?" I ask, hoping Liza has some sort of information.

"Oh, you mean the woman who darted out of here as if she saw a ghost? Um, what just happened?"

"Her name, Liza. What's her name?" I walk over to her desk,

raking all ten of my fingers through my hair—something I tend to do when I'm earnestly focused on a project.

"Belle with an E. Her name is Daniella Belle. Didn't she give you her résumé?"

I shake my head. "Nope. We didn't even make it that far into the interview. But I want—scratch that—I *need* her to be my personal assistant." I straighten my suit jacket and turn to head toward the doorway that leads to my office. "Find her please, Liza. Just find her," I direct, swiping my keycard to open the door.

"Okay. I'll certainly try my best. She does have my scarf, after all. Oh, and, Antonio?" Liza says, her voice timid.

"Yes, Liza?" I pivot to face her as I hold the door open.

"Just so you know, TMZ is reporting that you were on the Metro this morning and had a heated confrontation with another passenger. Something about a viral video they plan to post on their show this afternoon. Shall I forward this to Public Relations? I'm sure they've got you mixed up with someone else." She shrugs and smirks. "Like you'd ever take the train to work, right?"

WANT TO READ MORE?

TURN THE PAGE FOR THE BUY LINK!

ALSO BY JOSLYN WESTBROOK

Razzle My Dazzle Series

Cinderella-ish (Book 1)

Haute Couture (Book 2)

Princessa (Book 3)

Delectables In The City (A Sexy Chick Lit Series)

The Fifty-Two Week Chronicles (Book 1)

Coming January 2021

A Cupcake and A Gentleman (Book 2)

My Fake Fiancé

(A Mostly Sweet & Sexy

Rom-Com Series)

My Fake Billionaire Fiancé

Coming 2021

My Fake Celebrity Fiancé

My Fake Wedding Date Fiancé

My Fake College Professor Fiancé

ABOUT THE AUTHOR

Wife. Mom. Foodie. Fashion Junkie. RomCom Lover.

Author of romantic comedies and contemporary romance, Joslyn Westbrook's novels feature sassy heroines and the arrogant, dreamy heroes who sweep them off their feet. When she's not writing, Joslyn can be found binge watching Netflix, cooking, shopping, and spending time with her husband and children in sunny California.

Learn more about Joslyn Westbrook by following her on social media.